"Yo

she said in a shaky voice.

"That's right," he agreed affably. "No more than you're a lady. We both want the same thing. I'm just more honest than you."

"And what is it we both want?" she asked coolly, happy she was able to control the quaver in her voice.

"Why, each other, of course." A hint of a smile played at his sculpted lips.

Hot currents of desire shot through her body, but she valiantly tried to fight them. "You're mistaken, Cassidy. I'm not interested in having an affair with you." She turned to face him, still trembling, but knowing she had to prove she meant what she said.

"You're scared to death of me, Longford. You know if we ever went to bed together, you'd be lost." He smiled at her, his eyes knowing.

"Face it, lady," Cassidy continued softly. "We want each other."

Dear Reader:

Welcome! You hold in your hand a Silhouette Desire—your ticket to a whole new world of reading pleasure.

A Silhouette Desire is a sensuous, contemporary romance about passions, problems and the ultimate power of love. It is about today's woman—intelligent, successful, giving—but it is also the story of a romance between two people who are strong enough to follow their own individual paths, yet strong enough to compromise, as well.

These books are written by, for and about every woman that you are—wife, mother, sister, lover, daughter, career woman. A Silhouette Desire heroine must face the same challenges, achieve the same successes, in her story as you do in your own life.

The Silhouette reader is not afraid to enjoy herself. She knows when to take things seriously and when to indulge in a fantasy world. With six books a month, Silhouette Desire strives to meet her many moods, but each book is always a compelling love story.

Make a commitment to romance—go wild with Silhouette Desire!

Best,

Isabel Swift
Senior Editor & Editorial Coordinator

KATHERINE GRANGER
A Match Made in Heaven

Silhouette Desire

Published by Silhouette Books New York

America's Publisher of Contemporary Romance

SILHOUETTE BOOKS
300 East 42nd St., New York, N.Y. 10017

ISBN: 0-373-05452-1

First Silhouette Books printing October 1988

Printed in the U.S.A.

Books by Katherine Granger

Silhouette Desire

Ruffled Feathers #392
Unwedded Bliss #410
He Loves Me, He Loves Me Not #428
A Match Made in Heaven #452

KATHERINE GRANGER

had never read a romance until 1975, when a friend dumped a grocery bag filled with them in her living room and suggested she might enjoy them. Hooked with the very first one, Ms. Granger became a closet romance writer three years later. When she isn't writing, she teaches creative writing and composition at a community college and freshman composition at her alma mater. Katherine lives in Connecticut with her cat Barnaby. She enjoys movies, theater, golf, the Boston Red Sox, weekends at New England country inns and visits to Cape Cod.

One

The rain was coming down in torrents when Gina Longford rounded a curve in her low-slung sports car and almost careered into a man changing a flat tire on the side of the road. She applied her brakes and skidded to a perilous stop, her heart thudding, her green eyes glinting angrily.

Despite the weather, she was out of the car in a flash, and as she neared the car parked on the side of the road, the sound of low cursing pierced the curtain of torrential rain.

"Of all the rotten luck," the man was saying between colorful expletives. "Now. Today. Here!"

Gina came to a stop directly behind him and tapped her toe impatiently, trying to contain her anger by folding her arms over her immaculate designer raincoat. Rain thudded against the rim of the man's hat she'd crammed over her thick black hair. "Having a bit of a problem, are we?"

The man paused imperceptibly then continued tightening the lug nuts on the tire. A flattened tire lay on the ground at his feet, shredded beyond repair. "What's it to you?" he finally growled, his back to her. "You didn't almost get killed by a blasted blowout."

"No," she responded coolly, "but I *did* almost get killed when I came around that curve and nearly hit your car." She stopped tapping her toe and glared at his back. "Well?" she demanded. "Aren't you concerned with the danger you're in? I could have killed you, not to mention myself."

He sighed audibly and stood up, wiping his hands on a rag. "Lady," he said tiredly, "after the day I've had, I wouldn't give a damn if a whole fleet of trucks hit me." He still hadn't bothered to turn and look at her.

She arched a wry brow. Not only was he a fool, he was a total boor, she thought, while taking in the solid strength of his upper back and shoulders beneath his rain-soaked white shirt. His hair was dark but a bit too long for her taste. She liked her men tall and lean and immaculately groomed, and this man looked as if he wouldn't know what to do with a three-piece suit if it hit him. She let her gaze wander down his impressive frame, noting that his faded jeans revealed solidly muscled legs. She was appalled to feel her heartbeat accelerate. Hadn't she learned enough by now to know that tall, dark, heartbreakingly macho men like this were nothing but trouble?

She turned her acid gaze to his dilapidated car and suppressed a shudder. It was an extremely old sedan, riddled with rust, with a rear window patched with sodden cardboard and a metal fender resting precariously on the caved-in rear bumper.

"Lovely car," she said wryly. "A regular collector's item."

Turning, she found him looking at her. For just a second, her heart stopped beating. There was something dangerously primitive about him. His swarthy skin looked even

darker with the two-day-old stubble of black beard that
covered his strong jaw. He had a slightly crooked nose and
dark brows over eyes as dark and piercing as an eagle's.
Unconsciously she backed away. Power emanated from him
in dangerous eddies, so potent that she felt weak, as if he
were draining her energy to fuel his own anger.

For he *was* angry—she realized that now. Murderously
angry. She backed away again. At that moment, everything
became a blur. There was the sudden, jarring blast of a car's
horn, the glinting flash of headlights sweeping over her, then
she was being pulled rudely out of the path of the oncom-
ing car and swept against the man's powerful chest. For
seconds, she stayed in his embrace, registering the cold
dampness of his shirt, the strong beat of his heart under her
hand, the feel of his rocklike muscles, the faint scent of
musk, which might have been the remnants of after-shave.
Before she could sort it out, he took her by the upper arms
and shook her. Hard.

"You damned fool," he snarled. "You could have gotten yourself killed!"

He had dislodged her hat, freeing her thick, unruly hair,
which fell in ebony curls around her face and shoulders. She
heard his sharp intake of breath but shook her hair back and
glared at him dangerously as she retrieved her hat.

"You have a lot of nerve," she said in a low voice that
vibrated with anger. "You almost made me get killed, or kill
you—which probably would have been doing the world a
favor—and yet you have the nerve to call *me* a fool?" She
harrumphed haughtily, jammed her hat on her head, then
turned on her stylish heel and stalked back toward her car.

"Just like a woman," he called after her.

She whirled to face him. "What's that supposed to
mean?" she snapped. She was getting soaked but didn't
care; her anger was keeping her warm.

"Right when the fight starts to get interesting, you turn tail and run," he taunted.

She lifted her head, sensing a change in him. He was no longer so murderously angry. Though he still emanated danger, it was a different sort now. He was walking lazily toward her, as if the rain weren't pelting furiously from the heavens, his head tilted slightly, his eyes filled with derision. Because his shirt was soaked, she could see the dark mat of hair that swirled in dizzying circles on his powerful chest.

She sensed his interest and felt a raw thrill run through her, which she hastened to shake off. Throwing him a scornful look, she turned her back on him and said over her shoulder, "That's right. I'm afraid you're not worth fighting with."

"So you only go after men with tons of money, is that it?" he called.

She paused at her car and looked back in amusement. "Precisely," she said, then got in and drove off. As she roared away, she looked in her rearview mirror and saw him standing with his hands on his lean hips, watching. She let out a pent-up breath but was disgusted to find her fingers trembling.

After trying every station on the radio, she turned it off and listened instead to the steady drumming of rain on the car. The wipers were trying valiantly to clear the windshield, but they seemed to be waging a losing battle. She slowed down and took a deep breath.

She was nervous about her audition in New Haven this afternoon, that was the problem. Her sweaty palms and palpitating heart didn't have anything to do with the man she'd just left back there in the rain. Men weren't worth worrying about, especially men like him—unshaven, rude men who drove junk cars and probably expected women to cook them dinner and wash the dishes afterward, then engage in a pleasant little tumble in the hay.

She shuddered, remembering the beastly experience with her ex-husband, Jack. She'd had enough of the traditional male-female relationship to last ten lifetimes. She had a great job that had brought her professional respect and decent money. Now she was on her way to becoming famous. At least she would be if she ever got through this rain. Then all she would have to do was beat out the competition.

The reception room of the television network's New Haven affiliate station was filled with well-dressed men and one other woman. Gina took a deep breath to calm her nervous jitters and sat in one of the last empty chairs near the door. A movie reviewer for a Hartford newspaper, she'd appeared on a couple of television interview shows and had been guest host for a morning news program one week, but had never actually had a job in the field. Was that experience enough to help her land this job as on-air host for a half-hour syndicated movie-review program? Now, sitting in the waiting room, looking over the other candidates, who all appeared supremely confident, she felt her first real misgivings.

She glanced up from the magazine she was pretending to read and inconspicuously examined the other woman, who wore a navy blue suit, a light blue tailored blouse and a tiny scarf at her neck. The men all wore suits or sport coats and trousers. Sighing, she wondered if her short black knit dress and the black, hunter green and rust-colored paisley-print scarf she'd thrown over her shoulders were too bohemian. Thanks to her adventures in the rain a while ago, her cloud of black hair curled around her head in wild abandon, but there wasn't time to redo it or pin it on top of her head. She would just have to trust that her natural sense of style would come across on camera.

Just then, the door opened with a gust of wind, sending a stinging spray of rain over Gina and her magazine. She cast a brief, affronted look at the person who'd just come in, then simply stared.

It was him—the man with the flat tire. He'd put on a wool herringbone sport coat, but nothing could hide the fact that he was soaked to the skin. And anyway, she would never forget his face. It was as dark and unrelenting as it had been an hour ago in the rain, and he looked just as angry. He left his name with the receptionist, then found his way back to the only empty chair, which was next to Gina.

When he reached her, he did a double take. "You," he said, dropping wearily into the chair. "With the luck I've had today, I might have known you'd be coming to the same audition."

"With the luck you've had today," Gina answered flippantly, "you might as well leave now. You don't stand a chance. I'm getting the job."

He eased himself lower in the chair. "I find you assertive women so damned tiresome," he said with an air of mock pleasantry.

"Do you?" she answered sweetly. "Well, I find you macho men a bit tiresome, too."

"So we're even," he said, yawning. "Is there any coffee around, or do we all have to sit here like zombies until they call our names?"

She shrugged, flipping through the magazine, not even bothering to answer. He gave her a sour look and got up, disappearing down a long corridor. A few minutes later he reappeared, carrying two cups of coffee. He sat down, sipping from one cup and putting the other on the table between him and Gina.

"Oh, you shouldn't have," Gina said, reaching for the coffee.

"I didn't."

She looked up, startled. He lifted a dark eyebrow derisively. "It's for me. A second cup. If you want coffee, get your own."

She withdrew her hand as casually as she could. "No, thank you," she murmured, embarrassed at her assumption.

"You sure were willing to take it when you thought I'd bought it for you," he pointed out.

She ignored him, despite a red-hot urge to belt him. The man was the most odious human being—if one could charitably call him that—she'd ever had the displeasure of meeting.

"So," he continued. "I know this much about you: you don't stop to help a person in need, you stop to yell at him. You like rich men, and you expect the man to pay. Tell me, what's a high-class dame like you doing here, anyway? You can't be here for the job. Women like you make your living by marrying rich men. Or sleeping with them."

That did it. She slammed the magazine shut and faced him, her eyes flashing. "You are the most repugnant piece of refuse I have ever met. You jump to conclusions, judge people without any knowledge of the person you're judging—"

"Gina Longford?" called the receptionist.

Her tirade interrupted, Gina took a deep breath, smoothed her hand over her dress and stood up. "That's me," she said. "I don't suppose you'd want to wish me luck."

"That's right," he said pleasantly. "I wouldn't."

She lifted her chin and stalked off, wondering why she'd even said such a stupid thing in the first place.

At least her anger had lessened her nervousness. She went into the studio energized. Her cheeks were becomingly flushed, her eyes sparkled, and she delivered her three-minute critique of the latest Gene Harmon film with verve, zest and flair.

Or at least she thought so. The two interviewers merely asked her to wait in the reception room, without a word about how she'd done. Sitting in the rapidly emptying reception area, she couldn't resist nibbling on her thumbnail. Only three people were left, and one of them was that odious man. She'd found out his last name was Cassidy, but that's all she knew about him—other than that he was the most contemptible male she'd met in years. So far, he outdid her ex-husband, and that was saying something.

Finally, to keep from completely biting off her thumbnail, she picked up a magazine and succeeded in immersing herself in an absorbing article. A short while later, she was surprised to hear her name being called out.

"Ms. Longford?"

She looked up at the pretty receptionist. "Yes?"

"They'd like to see you in the studio again, Ms. Longford."

"They would?" She stared at the receptionist, afraid to believe it was good news she was getting.

"They would." The receptionist grinned at her. "You're one of the finalists."

"Oh, thank heavens," Gina said, letting out a deep breath of relief. "How many of us are there?"

"Just two."

"Oh..." Gina gulped, the full impact of the information reaching her stomach, which suddenly seemed to be filled with butterflies, all swirling and dancing, making her feel sick.

"Good luck," the young woman said, smiling encouragingly.

Gina smiled back and made her way to the studio. The two interviewers—a man and a woman—sat in canvas director's chairs, sipping coffee.

"Ms. Longford," said Peter Davis, the producer and director of the movie-review show, "have a seat. We were impressed with your delivery. You seem to have a flair for television."

Gina smiled warmly. "Well, I've done quite a few guest appearances and I spent a week subbing for Dolly Saunders." She knew the mention of Dolly Saunders would help, since Dolly was the best-known television host in Connecticut.

Phyllis Thompson, the executive vice president of the network for programming, spoke up. "We'd like to watch you again. Have you got another critique you could do?"

"Yes, I came prepared," Gina said with a smile. She made her way to the chair in front of the camera and took a deep breath. When they signaled her, she began. "We've all been waiting for the new Walter Humphries film for three years," she said, "and it's finally out. Personally, I'd have preferred to wait another year or two, because this new film is abominable—"

From beyond the circle of lights there came a loud snort of contemptuous laughter. "Abominable?" a deep voice male asked unbelievingly. "How can you say that?"

Gina stared, dumbstruck. She put a hand up to shade her eyes, trying to see who could be so rude as to interrupt her audition. From the shadows, a tall, well-built masculine form appeared. "You really believe that?" questioned the man she'd come to detest. "You really think this film is bad?" he asked, prodding her again.

She swallowed a fireball of anger but couldn't keep the wrath from her voice. "You're damned right I do," she snapped. "This is the worst film I've seen all year." It wasn't, of course, but then he seemed to have that effect on her.

"You can't be serious," Cassidy whooped. "It's his best film since his masterpiece, *Durango*."

"Well, there you have it!" she said, throwing her hands up as if that explained everything. "Anyone who thinks *Durango* is a masterpiece hasn't the taste to distinguish good from bad." She smiled sweetly. "Now would you kindly shut up? I'm interviewing for a job here."

"So am I," Cassidy shot back. "And as far as I'm concerned, this is war. And you know what they say about love and war."

She nodded slowly, taking his measure more fully. He might be dressed like a bum, but there was something about him that commanded attention. Perhaps she should take him more seriously as a contender. "Yes, as a matter of fact, I do," she said quietly. "All's fair in love and war. Or so they say."

"That's right. I'm challenging you, Ms. Longford. You better shine, honey, or this job is mine."

Gina glanced at the interviewers but saw only calculated interest on their faces. Neither made a move to come to her aid. She realized suddenly she was in a tank of piranhas. People had told her television was a competitive field, but she'd pooh-poohed the idea. Journalism was competitive, too, or so she'd thought until now. Suddenly journalism looked like nursery school compared to working in television.

She took a deep breath and faced the camera again. "As I was saying, Walt Humphries should have taken another year to reedit this abysmal failure. He calls his new film

Summer Wine, but I think he should have spelled that 'whine,' because that's the tone he maintains throughout this schlocky, desperate attempt to put the cause of women's liberation back three generations.''

"I might have known," Cassidy interrupted from the sidelines. "Trust a woman not to get the meaning of a Walter Humphries film."

"Trust a man not to see what Walter Humphries is doing," she retorted, then went on without missing a beat. "*Summer Wine* is the same old boy-meets-girl, loses-girl, wins-girl story that's kept Hollywood rolling in money since filmmaking began. In the hands of a more sensitive director, it could have been a fresh, innovative statement about male-female relationships today. In the hands of Walt Humphries, we get the same tired old clichés, endless close-ups of lovers embracing, the soft, sweet swell of a fabulous Ted Lazenby score, and some pretty good performances by Laura Andrews and Peter Simon. Those performances redeem *Summer Wine* to an extent, but my final recommendation is to stay home and watch a *Durango* rerun on cable. You'll get a better Walter Humphries film and save ten bucks in the bargain."

"And my recommendation is to see *Summer Wine*," Cassidy said, walking onto the set, pulling a canvas director's chair behind him. He slumped into it opposite Gina and crossed his feet at the ankles, fixing her with steady dark eyes. "You missed the entire point, Longford," Cassidy said. "Walter Humphries is telling us that women's liberation isn't working. It's separating men and women, not bringing them closer."

"Rubbish!" Gina said heatedly. "If he'd been saying that, I'd have respected his right to his own opinion, but he doesn't even have a coherent theme in this picture. *Summer Wine* starts out with a promise and ends on a whimper." She shook her head in disgust and prepared to get up, but Cassidy reached out and took her hand to keep her from leaving.

"At least have the courtesy to stay and listen to my opinion," he commanded.

Startled, she sank back in her chair, looking nervously at the two interviewers. They didn't move from their chairs, so she shrugged and sat back. "Okay," she said, placing her elbows on the arms of the chair and lacing her fingers together, "go ahead. I can hardly wait to hear it. If it's as informed as the rest of what you're saying, our viewers will be howling with laughter."

Cassidy just smiled lazily. "Gina," he said softly, suddenly changing his approach. "Listen to Colin Cassidy. Ol' Colin knows what he's talking about."

Gina stared into his eyes, feeling delicate shivers travel over her skin. When he talked softly like that, he mesmerized her. She felt her heart begin to pound, felt her breathing begin to quicken. For some reason, she couldn't take her eyes off him. She felt as if she were being seduced in front of the camera, but she was helpless to stop it from happening.

Then his words pierced the haze that surrounded her, and she began to chuckle. "You're kidding!" she said when he was finished. "What'd Walt Humphries do? Slip you a twenty to give him a favorable review?"

"Are you insinuating I'd take a bribe?" Colin asked.

"No, since you missed the point of the movie, I assume that if Humphries handed you a twenty, you'd probably miss that point too and think he owed it to you or something." She shook her head scornfully and rose from her chair.

"Ms. Longford," Peter Davis said from the sidelines. "Would you sit down, please?"

Faltering, Gina sank back into her chair. She had gotten so riled by Colin Cassidy's interruption that she'd momentarily forgotten this was an audition. As the two interviewers whispered heatedly on the sidelines, Gina felt despair flood through her. This awful man had purposely baited her and ruined her chances. He'd come steamrolling in from the shadows, intentionally trying to make her look bad.

Then she brightened. Maybe his strategy had backfired. Maybe his rudeness had simply made *him* look bad in the eyes of the interviewers. Gina sat up, feeling hope rise within her.

"Mr. Cassidy?" Peter Davis said.

"Yes?"

"You're hired."

Gina felt her hopes fall. She slumped in her chair, closing her eyes against the bright lights. For a moment, she just sat there, sunk in misery, then she slowly rallied and stood up.

"Just a moment, Ms. Longford," Peter Davis said.

"That's okay," she answered, managing a good-natured grin. "I know when I've lost."

"But you haven't lost, Ms. Longford," he said, grinning back at her. "You stood up to Colin with admirable courage. We liked that. Your courage impressed us. In fact, we like the way you two work together. You send up sparks. You're hired, too, Ms. Longford. From now on, you and Colin Cassidy are a team."

Two

A team?'' Gina echoed disbelievingly, sinking back into her chair. "We'd kill each other!"

"Well, we can only hope," Peter said, smiling enigmatically.

Gina stared. "I don't get it," she said, looking from Peter Davis to Phyllis Thompson. "Colin Cassidy and I wouldn't last two minutes on the same program together. Anybody can see that."

"Gina," Phyllis said, "that's what makes terrific television—surprise, the unanticipated. You two had us in the palms of your hands. We were enthralled. And if we've learned one thing, it's this: what interests us, interests our viewers. You two are dynamite together, literally as well as figuratively. Welcome aboard, Ms. Longford. Drop around to the manager's office later and we'll have a contract ready for the two of you to sign."

"But—" Gina hesitated, looking miserably from one to the other. She felt like a kitten facing a pit bull terrier.

"You mean you don't want the job?" Phyllis asked.

Gina glanced anxiously at Colin Cassidy. He merely raised his eyebrows at her, slumped deeper into his chair, crossed his long, muscular legs and put his head back as if he were going to sleep.

"Wake up, Cassidy," she snapped. "You got me into this mess—get me out of it."

He raised his head and smiled lazily. "The job's mine if you don't take the offer. Personally, I'd be delighted if you back out."

"Don't be so sure of yourself, Mr. Cassidy," Phyllis said. "You two work great together. You're a team. If Ms. Longford backs out, you're out too. We'll start our search all over again."

Colin sat bolt upright. "What'd you say?"

"You heard me," Phyllis said, turning back to Gina. "So what's the story, Ms. Longford? Are you taking our offer?"

Gina looked from Phyllis to Peter to Colin, then back to Phyllis. "Let me get this straight. If I refuse, Colin loses out, too. Does that mean you don't want me without him, either?"

"That's right. It's the two of you together or neither one of you. Tell you what, we'll leave you alone and let you talk it over. I realize this is unexpected, so take a few minutes to discuss it."

"A few minutes!" Gina exclaimed. "This is our future we're talking about here!"

Phyllis shrugged. "Okay, so have a cup of coffee together. Be back in half an hour with your decision."

"Half an hour," Gina grumbled as she and Colin walked down the deserted corridor toward the coffee machine.

"They've got us shackled together like prisoners, just like that old movie."

"Which one are you?" Colin asked drowsily. "Tony Curtis or Sidney Poitier?"

She glared at him, put fifty cents in the machine and was rewarded with a cup that came out sideways. Half her coffee splashed over her and half landed in the cup. "Great," she said sarcastically. "Half a cup of coffee for fifty lousy cents and a laundry bill for ten dollars."

"Join the crowd. Today's been the worst day of my life. You've just crowned it."

"Me?" Gina retorted. "What have I got to do with it? If you hadn't had the bright idea of horning in on my audition, this wouldn't have happened."

"Look, I need this job. I just got fired, my roommate moved out on me and my car broke down. Humor me, okay?"

Gina turned her back on him, trembling with anger. "Humor you," she finally said, bristling. "Of all the nervy, egotistical, rude, overbearing—"

"All right," he said wearily. "I get the picture."

"Are you always this laid-back?" she asked, peering at him. He was leaning against the wall, his head back, his eyes closed. He looked utterly at ease.

"This isn't laid-back, honey, this is near-death. I've just spent two days driving halfway cross-country to get to this damned audition, only to have you screw it up for me."

"Me?" she shrieked.

"Stop!" he said, holding a hand to his head.

Seeing the look on his face, Gina immediately swallowed her tirade. "What's the matter? Are you okay?"

He groaned and slowly opened his eyes. "No, I am *not* okay. I am falling-down dead tired. I have a headache the size of a Mack truck and no money. I am down, and I am out. Things have never been worse. Say you'll take the damn job, or I'm sunk."

"This isn't fair," Gina said, her voice shaking. "I am not responsible for you, Mr. Cassidy. If you can't keep a job, that's not my problem. It is just not fair for you to lay this on me."

"Oh, shut up," he said tiredly. "Life's not fair, okay?" He took a sip of coffee and rubbed his temples, then squeezed the bridge of his nose. "Okay, you're right. I apologize. I shouldn't lay my problems on you. Fine. Don't take the offer. I'll find a job. I'm not *that* hard up."

Gina peered at him. "Where will you stay? You said you don't have any money."

He shrugged. "I'll sleep in the car. That's how I managed the past two nights."

"That's totally ridiculous," Gina said. "You can't sleep in a *car*."

"Honey," he said, sighing heavily. "I just did. For two nights. Just make up your mind, huh?"

"Don't call me honey," she snapped. "I can't stand it when a man calls me honey."

"Probably because you realize the name doesn't in any way fit," he sniped.

She glared at him, then sipped her coffee. "Maybe we can work something out."

"Like what? Write it in our contracts that no knives or guns be allowed on the set?"

"Will you be serious just once?" she demanded.

He shrugged and sipped his coffee, not bothering to respond.

Gina bit her lip and began to pace back and forth. "How long would the contract be for?"

"Probably only half a season, maybe less. The networks don't like to put out good money on a show that hasn't proved itself. Maybe they'd sign us for eight shows, something like that, just to test the waters.''

"What do you think? Could we stand each other that long?''

He shrugged. "I need the money, Longford. I can stand anyone for that long if I have to. Even you.'' He paused. "I think.''

"You're impossible. I'm trying to be serious about this, Cassidy, and you're making sarcastic jokes.''

"It's a character flaw,'' he said. "Get used to it.''

"That's just it—I don't know if I can. You set my teeth on edge. You make me want to scream. I—'' She stared at him, frowning, realizing the full extent of the problem. "I just don't like you, Mr. Cassidy.''

"Yeah?'' he asked, chuckling softly. "How come? Most women like me quite a bit.''

For a minute, she almost saw what he meant, then she shook off her impression. "It's your ego,'' she said flatly. "I can't stand men with inflated egos.''

He chuckled lazily, then pushed away from the wall. "So, what gives? Are we on or what?''

She drained the last of the coffee from her cup, crumpled it and tossed it into a garbage can. "Against my better judgment, I think we are.''

"Longford,'' he said, breaking into a grin. "I could kiss you for that.''

"Don't even think about it,'' she warned, putting out a hand to ward him off. "I mean that, Cassidy. I dislike you intensely, but I want this job. Because it's so important to me, I'm willing to give it a chance. Just keep your distance. Come closer than five feet and I'll deck you. Is that clear?''

"As transparent as plate glass.''

"Good. Just remember it."

He grinned at her. "My headache's disappearing."

"Amazing what the thought of a contract can do, isn't it?" she asked dryly.

His grin widened, but he didn't say another word.

Two hours later, they had negotiated their price upward, signed their contracts and were standing in the reception area, staring out at the rain.

"Are you really going to sleep in that car?" Gina asked doubtfully.

Colin shrugged. "They wouldn't give me any money up front, so I guess I'll have to."

Gina stared glumly at his car. If possible, it looked even worse than it had when she'd first seen it. "Why did you leave the side window down?" she asked suddenly. "The front seat will be soaked."

"There isn't a side window," he replied. "Believe me, if there were, I wouldn't have left it down."

"How long have you had this...this...thing?"

"Eighteen hours, I think." He scratched his chin thoughtfully and nodded. "Yup, eighteen hours."

She stared at him as if he were from Mars. "Do you always keep a car that long?" she asked sarcastically.

"My car broke down. I had to buy this one for two hundred bucks." He sighed. "Just another event in the long string of bad luck in my life."

She was almost moved to pity but resisted firmly. "You can't sleep in that car tonight, Cassidy," she said sternly, disliking him even more now that he was proving human.

"I have to, Longford."

She stared at the car indecisively, then pulled out her wallet. "Look, here's—" she counted her money "—fifteen dollars."

"That might get me a room in an alley," he said.

She bit her lip, trying frantically to come up with a solution to his problem. "I could lend you my credit card."

"Yeah, but then I'd have to learn to forge your signature. And then there's the part about wearing a dress and a wig and makeup." He shook his head. "Sorry, it was kind of you to offer, but I don't think it'd work."

She stared miserably at his car. "You *can't* sleep in that car, Cassidy."

"You got a better idea?"

She debated, and finally fairness won. "Yes. You'll have to sleep with me."

His eyebrows went up. She glared at him. "At my house. Alone. Not *with* me," she said from between clenched teeth.

"I'm glad you clarified things. For a while, I thought you were making a pass at me."

"That will never happen in a million years, Cassidy. You aren't my type, in any way, shape or form."

"Just who is?"

"You say that as if you think I'm not interested in any men."

"Are you?"

She looked away from his laughing eyes. "I date, if that's what you're asking, but I'm not interested in intimate relationships. I had one once and it ended disastrously. I learned to steer clear of men. Men and I are like oil and water—we don't mix."

"Did you marry the guy?"

"Yes. Unfortunately."

"How long did it last?"

"Two years. Then I wised up and got out."

"Meaning you decided all male development stopped with the Neanderthal, right?"

"Meaning I got tired of his fooling around with everything in skirts. Meaning I got tired of cooking and cleaning and scrubbing while he sat on his behind and watched football. Meaning I got smart, period."

"Subject's closed, I take it."

"Correct."

"Okay," he said. "I'll sleep at your place."

"Fine," she said. "Tomorrow I'll write you a check. It's a loan, Cassidy, understand? You'll repay me when you get your first paycheck. Is that clear?"

"Perfectly."

"If it weren't too late to get to a bank, I'd write you one now," she said, buttoning her coat and preparing to dash to her car.

"You don't have to explain. I know you're not interested in my body tonight." He tilted his head sideways. "Are you?"

"I most certainly am not."

"I thought so."

"Just don't try to slip into my bedroom tonight, Cassidy, or you'll be singing soprano for the rest of your life."

"Honey, sleeping with you is the farthest thing from my mind," he said pleasantly. "I'd rather sleep with a shark."

"I'd rather you slept with a shark, too," she said sweetly, "so that makes two of us. Are you ready?"

"Want me to follow you?"

"Well, considering you don't know where I live, I guess it'd be kind of difficult to drive in front of me, wouldn't it?" she remarked, again with saccharine sweetness.

"Sharp," he said, raising his eyebrows. "Very sharp, that tongue of yours."

She turned her back on him and raced to her car, but when she drove up beside him, he was slumped comfortably in his car. She rolled down her window and shouted at him, "What's the matter? You too tired to drive?"

"Nope," he said cheerfully, "I'm out of gas."

She sat and stared at him, wondering how on earth any man could be so utterly irritating. Everything he did set her teeth on edge, and here she was offering him the chance to sleep at her house. She was most definitely certifiable. "Get in," she ordered. "Don't talk, just get in and sit there. Quietly. If you say one word, I'll put you out on the side of the road and let you fend for yourself."

He reached in the back of his car for his suitcase, then sprinted to her car and wedged the bag behind the seat. "What makes you think I'd *want* to talk with you?" he asked when he got in.

She rolled her eyes and put the car into gear. "You're impossible."

"You bring out the best in me."

"If this is the best, I'd hate to see the worst."

"Oh, you will, Longford," he said, sliding down in the plush leather seat and smiling to himself. "We're a team, remember? You'll see all sides of me before long."

"That's what I'm afraid of," she said, maneuvering the car into traffic.

"Where do you live?"

"In the backwoods, as far from civilization as I can get," she replied. "It's only a little place, but I'm comfortable. There's a guest room, a study, a living room and a kitchen. It's...cozy...and also convenient. It's not too far from Long Island Sound, and even on a bad traffic day, I can get to Hartford within an hour. I don't have regular hours at the paper, so commuting isn't all that bad."

"Where do you work?"

"*The Telegram*," she answered. "But my column's syndicated. Maybe you've read it—'Lens on Hollywood' by G. S. Longford."

He sat up slowly, his face blank. "You can't be," he said.

"I can't be what?"

He sank down in the seat with a groan. "I don't believe it. You're G. S. Longford, the syndicated movie reviewer."

"I just *said* that," she said irritably. "And what's wrong with it, anyway? I suppose you hate my columns."

"I always thought G. S. Longford was a guy," he said with wonder, then began to chuckle as if the joke were on him. "I like your work, for the most part. I never agree with you, of course, but I like the way you write."

She smiled wryly. One point for her. "Where are you from, Cassidy?"

"New Mexico. I was at the *Desert Inquirer* in Albuquerque."

"But you got fired. At least that's what I think you said."

He closed his eyes and folded his arms. "Uh-huh."

"How come?" she asked, not willing to be put off by his sudden quiet. "Circulation low? Did they lay off some staff?"

"Nope," he said, sounding as if he hadn't a care in the world. "I just got canned. Let that be a lesson to you, Longford. Don't sleep with the publisher's daughter—or in your case, son. When things don't work out, they take sweet revenge."

"You don't sound too heartbroken. What'd she do? Wise up and throw you out?"

He stiffened, then shrugged, looking a little too careless to Gina's way of thinking. If she didn't know better, she'd almost think this bear had a heart. "She walked, all right," he admitted. "But then it didn't really matter. Sally and I didn't have very much in common, except in bed."

Gina struck her forehead with the palm of her hand. "I don't believe you said that!" she said. "That is so sexist! No *wonder* she moved out!"

"It's not sexist, Longford," he said shortly. "It's more than that. I think I'm a genuine, dyed-in-the-wool misogynist. I really don't like women."

Slowing down for a red light, she turned to look at him, genuinely troubled by his tone of voice. "Why? What'd women ever do to you?"

He moved uncomfortably in his seat, as if bored with the entire conversation. "Oh, it's nothing personal. I just don't like women."

"But..." She stared at him, frowning. "Something must have caused you to feel this way. Someone must have hurt you...."

He turned his head and fixed her with steely eyes. "Don't ask, Longford, okay? Don't even ask."

Something in his tone told her he wasn't fooling. She nodded and looked back at the road. They drove in silence awhile, then she said, "This isn't going to work. You know that, don't you, Cassidy?"

"It'll have to work. I need the money and you want the job."

"But we . . . we dislike each other."

"So? You heard what that Thompson woman said—we're dynamite together. We'll capitalize on it. Who knows, maybe it'll be fun."

"Fun," she said glumly. "Turning our intense dislike for one another into televised entertainment." She sighed. "Fun."

"You have misgivings?"

"I've had misgivings from the very moment I agreed to this farce."

"Then back out if you're worried. I'll find another job."

She pulled off the highway and headed down the curving country road where she'd almost run into him this morning. "How come you were on this road, anyway?" she asked suddenly.

"I got lost. I told you, it was a rotten day. I took the wrong turn off the highway and ended up on this road. Don't ask about everything else that happened to me. You wouldn't believe any of it. If there's a Bad Luck god, he's been on my case the past few years."

"Okay." She was silent a moment. "Still, it's kind of a coincidence that you were on this road, and I stopped, and then we went to the same audition and ended up working together, isn't it?"

He shrugged. "Put like that it is, I guess."

"What other way could I put it?" she asked dryly.

"Look at it this way: if you hadn't stopped, you'd have never known I was on this road, right?"

She frowned. "Right."

"So? If you'd never known, it wouldn't seem like a coincidence."

"But—" She frowned harder, trying to fathom his logic. Finally she gave up. "Oh, never mind. I don't suppose it's important."

"That's right, it isn't." He burrowed lower in the seat and closed his eyes.

"Don't get too comfortable, Cassidy," she said. "We're almost home."

He opened his eyes and sat up. "All I see is woods."

"I told you I live in the country. There's lots of woods in Connecticut."

"I can see that."

She slowed and turned into a rutted dirt road, now a sea of mud. She drove at three miles an hour in first gear, squishing through the mud and praying she wouldn't get stuck.

"How far off the beaten path do you live?" he asked, his voice sharp with sarcasm. "Up around Alaska somewhere?"

They rounded a curve. Up ahead, a small stone cottage sat in a clearing. "It's not quite as far as Alaska, Cassidy."

"Okay, let's call it Montana."

"I call it home," she said gently, coming to a stop. "And tonight, because you are a lucky person and because I have a heart of gold, you'll call it home, too."

"Don't bet on it," he said, casting her a grim look. "I'm not a domesticated animal. I hate cozy and I hate cute. Got that? I like dirty socks on the floor and dirty dishes in the sink."

"Then you're going to be utterly miserable here," she replied breezily, cramming her hat on her head and flinging open the door.

"I could have told you that already," Colin said under his breath.

She heard him but refused to respond. Instead, she ran toward the house through the pelting rain, dodging puddles and spattering mud everywhere, wondering what on earth had ever possessed her to invite this irredeemable male into her home.

Three

———

Gina shoved some crumpled newspaper under the logs in the fireplace, then struck a match and lit the fire. Soon the pleasant aroma of apple logs and woodsmoke filled the living room, chasing away the chill. As she lit a lamp, Colin appeared in the doorway. He was drying his hair with a towel, and she saw that he'd shaved and changed into an old Dallas Cowboys T-shirt that molded his muscular chest, and faded jeans that rode low on his lean hips.

Gina felt a frightening sensation in the pit of her stomach. She knew what it meant—she was physically attracted to the reprobate. Her head might know he was nothing but trouble, but her ornery glands insisted on responding to him. But she'd given up obeying the urgings of her body long ago. She could handle the situation. She was a mature adult and didn't relish the thought of getting involved with a man straight out of the Stone Age. But here he was, and suddenly her little house seemed no bigger than a match-box.

"Well, Mr. Cassidy," she said breezily, "I see you found the bathroom all right."

He halted his slow perusal of her living room and glanced at her. "I did."

She looked away from him, remembering the congenial clutter of soaps, lotions and cosmetics that filled the small bathroom between her room and the guest room. It made her suddenly uncomfortable to think of Colin Cassidy showering in her private bath, looking over all of her most personal possessions, moving them aside to make room for his more masculine paraphernalia....

To chase away her discomfort, she looked around the living room, wondering how it appeared to him. From the moment she'd first seen the little cottage, she'd fallen in love with it. It had character, charm and warmth. The stucco walls were whitewashed, but overhead the exposed rafters were deep chocolate brown. The living room was two steps down from the stone-paved foyer, and large Oriental rugs covered most of the polished wood floor, their burgundy and navy colors muted now, adding to the comfort of the room.

A white couch heaped with navy and burgundy pillows faced the fireplace. Behind it, an antique pine trestle table held dozens of books about art, gardening and movies. A pair of wing chairs nestled near the fireplace. The entire side wall consisted of small-paned windows, in the middle of which French doors opened onto a small stone-paved patio.

"Do you like it, Mr. Cassidy?" Gina asked.

He shrugged and dropped his towel on a chair. "It'll do," he said, then seemed to realize that Gina was livid. Apologizing, he picked up the towel, then looked around. "Well, where should I put it?"

"Try the hamper," she suggested semisweetly, then turned on her heel and stalked off to the kitchen.

A second later, Colin Cassidy appeared right behind her, the damp towel in his hands. "I'm sorry," he said, "but you have to understand—I live like a slob. I *like* living like a slob."

"Fine," she said shortly, "just don't live like one when you're around me."

Colin's eyes sparkled defiantly as he wadded up the towel. "Okay, just where is this hamper?"

"In the bathroom, Mr. Cassidy," she retorted coolly. "Where would you expect it to be?"

"At your house?" he asked with mock sweetness. "Why, I'd expect you to have one or two in every room."

"Very funny," she said tightly, examining the contents of the refrigerator. "Tell me, would you rather cook or clean up afterward?"

"Oh, I get it," he said darkly. "This is a quick one-night lesson in domesticity, right Longford? You're going to straighten me out and teach me to be liberated, or some such thing, is that it?"

"Mr. Cassidy," Gina said, turning slowly, "you are a guest in my home for the night. I don't want you here, but circumstances forbade me to be impolite. So, we're stuck together like two peas in a pod." She took a deep breath in an effort to calm down, but when she continued, her voice rose despite her best efforts to remain cool. "Surely you don't expect me to *wait* on you?"

"Wouldn't you wait on any other guest?"

That stumped her. She stared at him a moment, then her anger had a chance to regroup. "No!" Whirling around, she started taking food from the refrigerator. "We'll have a salad,'' she said tightly, trying to rein in her temper, ''and an omelet.''

''A salad and eggs?'' he said incredulously from behind her.

She turned slowly, murder in her eyes. ''What's wrong with that?''

''I have driven five hundred miles today,'' he said, stabbing the air with his finger as if to underline his words. ''I got lost twice, dropped a couple of hundred dollars on useless repairs to my engine, then had to junk my own car and buy that piece of scrap metal back at the station. I have weathered rain, lightning, hail and a blown-out tire—'' He broke off suddenly, as if reconsidering what he'd been about to say, then began again, full tilt. ''I ate a candy bar for breakfast and a handful of nuts for lunch, and you want to feed me *eggs*?''

Gina's face remained impassive. ''Would half a dozen suffice?'' She started taking eggs out of the refrigerator, slamming them down on the counter. One by one they broke, splattering the counter, the refrigerator and her. At last she banged the refrigerator shut and looked back at him. ''Are you satisfied, Mr. Cassidy? Are things messy enough for you now?'' With that, she turned and stomped toward the door, totally aghast at her behavior, but unable to stop herself.

''You are a shrew, Longford,'' he called after her.

She looked back. ''And you, Mr. Cassidy, are a swine.'' Then she smiled sweetly. ''Oh, and when you're finished with the eggs, would you be kind enough to clean up?''

She paused only long enough to see the look of dark anger on his face, then she slammed the door behind her and hurried toward the sanctuary of her bedroom. She was cold and she was wet. The top half of her was splattered with eggs and the bottom half with mud. She felt like a bedraggled cat. She needed a bath, desperately. Perhaps after soaking in a hot tub for a while, she could face the rest of the evening with her unwelcome guest.

But when she reached the bathroom, her temper soared. Chaos reigned. Her cosmetics and lotions had indeed been pushed aside, making room for a plethora of male junk: a razor, a pack of blades, a can of shaving cream, deodorant, after-shave, and a styptic pencil.

But that was the least of it. The bathroom was full of puddles, two towels lay discarded on the floor, and the remains of his whiskers were in the sink. His clothing lay scattered in a messy trail, as if he'd simply dropped each item as it came off en route from the guest room. Slowly she followed the trail backward, bending to pick up each item, starting with his undershorts, which lay in a puddle next to the ancient claw-footed tub, then his undershirt, back to his socks, then his trousers. She found his shirt on the floor in the guest room.

She had no sooner picked it up when the door opened and he appeared. "You are a nosy broad," he said. "This *is* my room, you know. I'd appreciate it if you'd stay out."

"Your room?" she said in a low voice. "*Your* room?" She looked around and began to laugh, feeling the beginnings of what felt suspiciously like hysteria building up in her. His suitcase was on the bed, its contents sprawling from it carelessly. His sport coat hung listlessly on the bedpost. His shoes lay on the floor, discarded as freely as the rest of his clothing. A pile of newspapers had been thrown next to his shoes, along with a ripped road map and two candy bar wrappers. The wastebasket, she noticed, was immaculate.

"You're a pig," she said in a low voice. "Without any help you've turned my lovely guest room into a sty in five minutes. How did you do it, Mr. Cassidy? Is this a skill you learned on your own, or did someone teach you?" She paused only long enough to catch her breath, then went on, her voice rising, her face getting red. "Someone had to teach you. Who was it? Your father? Surely it wasn't your mother! No woman on earth could make a mess like this!"

As she spoke, Colin's face had grown progressively darker. When she finished, he looked as angry as he had on the road earlier that day. "No, Ms. Longford," he said, his voice surprisingly quiet. "My mother didn't teach me. She was too busy—" He broke off abruptly, then thrust a distracted hand through his hair. Suddenly his mood changed. His anger diminished, replaced by icy reserve. "I'm sorry if my habits annoy you, but I'll be out of here tomorrow. After that you can return to your pristine existence. Will that do, Ms. Longford? Can you hold out for just one night?"

Puzzled, Gina stared at him. What had he been about to say about his mother? She realized she had somehow hit a nerve, and he'd only just kept himself from responding to that direct hit. "Yes, Mr. Cassidy," she said slowly, "I believe I can manage for one night."

"Good," he said, then turned and left the room, closing the door softly behind him.

Gina stared at the door, then slowly and mechanically went about straightening his room. She folded his clothes, hung his sport coat on a hanger to dry, put his shoes in the closet, closed his suitcase and deposited it in the closet next to his shoes. She threw the newspaper and candy wrappers in the wastebasket and folded the ripped road map and put it on the bedside table. The whole time she pondered what he was about to say about his mother—that she was too busy to teach him neatness? Too sick? Too tired?

Gina smoothed a hand over the quilt on the pencil-post bed, then impulsively turned back the covers and plumped the pillows. She went into her bedroom and found a few magazines and an old copy of *Huckleberry Finn* and put them on the table next to his bed. She glanced out the window, wishing she could cut some chrysanthemums to put in his room, but the rain had drenched them and they looked much too bedraggled to cheer up the room. When she had guests, she liked to pamper them, but today she would have to forgo flowers. Perhaps to compensate, she would make a steaming pot of tea or hot chocolate and sneak it in here tonight before he retired.

Bemused, Gina walked from Cassidy's room. She really was a puzzle. Just moments ago, she couldn't stand Cassidy, could barely wait for him to leave, and yet here she was now trying to figure out a way to make his short stay pleasant....

Gina showered quickly and changed into her usual at-home attire—jeans and a soft white peasant blouse. In the kitchen, she found Colin munching on cheese and crackers and drinking a beer. The eggs had been clumsily cleaned up, but a sticky residue remained on the counters. Still, she tried to keep her temper.

"Happy hour?" she asked.

"Supper," he said.

"Really, Mr. Cassidy, if you're that ignorant about cooking eggs, I'll make them for you myself."

"I'm not ignorant about cooking, Ms. Longford," he said coolly. "I just don't do it. On principle."

"Which principle is that, Mr. Cassidy?" she retorted. "The principle of pride or the principle of foolishness?"

He cast her a dark look and took a swig of beer, ignoring her. Sighing, she set about making herself a salad and an omelet. As the odor of butter sizzling in the frying pan pervaded the air, she turned to Colin. "Sure you won't have something?"

He looked as hungry as a puppy at the pound, but he shook his head obstinately. "No, thanks. Not hungry." Pushing his chair back, he got up and walked out of the room, the half-empty bottle of beer in his hand.

Gina stood with a hand on her hip, staring after him. Of all the cussed men! Frowning, she turned back to the stove and finished making herself an omelet. It lay plump and golden in the frying pan. As she stared down at it, she knew she couldn't eat it. She scooped it onto a plate next to some tossed salad and placed the plate on a wicker tray. She added a blue-and-white plaid napkin and tiny salt and pepper shakers. Hurrying, she got another beer from the refrigerator and poured it into a tall pilsner glass, then carried the tray to the living room.

She found Colin slumped on the couch, staring moodily out at the rain. Silently she placed the tray on the coffee table in front of him. "Here's some supper if you'd like it, Cassidy," she said, then turned without another word and went back to the kitchen.

She was still scouring the kitchen counter when the door opened and Colin appeared, carrying the tray with its empty plate and beer glass. "I decided to eat it since you went to the trouble of cooking it," he said grumpily, putting it down on the counter.

"Did you?" she asked noncommittally. She continued to clean, refusing to look up. She wasn't about to get into another spat with Cassidy. His inability to even thank her for the trouble she went to irritated her, but she was determined not to show it.

"It was even good," he said at last.

"Oh?" She rinsed the sponge and went back to scouring the counter.

The kitchen was silent for a couple of minutes, then he cleared his throat and said, "I've never had an omelet before. It's kind of like scrambled eggs, isn't it?"

She frowned at an egg speck she'd missed, then said absently, "Yes, I suppose it is at that."

"Just more compressed," Colin said, "instead of loose and fluffy."

"Mmm."

Again silence descended and the only sound that marred the quiet was the squeak of Gina's sponge on the immaculate counters.

"You've done that spot twice already," Colin finally pointed out.

Slowly Gina raised her eyes to his. "Oh." She rinsed the sponge again and began to attack his dishes, clattering the knife and fork into the stainless-steel sink and slamming the tray into its appointed slot in the cabinet.

"You sound angry," Colin said.

"How can a person sound angry without even speaking?" Gina asked icily.

"By banging everything in sight," he answered.

That did it. She turned around, her eyes spitting fire. "I went to the trouble of fixing your supper and I get not a word of thanks. Then you have the unmitigated gall to stand around and watch me clean the counters and haven't the common *courtesy* to do your own dishes."

"I said it was good," he protested.

"And that's as far as you can go, isn't it, Cassidy?" she said, angry that her voice was shaking. "You couldn't go the extra mile and thank me, could you?"

"That's right, Longford, I couldn't," he snapped. "Why the hell should I? Give a woman a compliment and she'll use it against you every time."

She stared at him, aghast. Was that how he felt? Did he mistrust all women so much that he instantly categorized them all as untrustworthy and irredeemable? She felt her spirits plummet, felt an unexplainable tiredness wash over her. "Just leave, Mr. Cassidy," she said wearily. "Go sprawl in comfort in the living room, or go to your room and see if you can make another mess. You and I are clearly at cross purposes. It's plain we'll never get along. This entire idea of cohosting the television program is absurd. We'll never get through the first taping, much less three months' worth of programs."

"We'll get through it because we have to," he said harshly. "You're not finking out on me now, Longford. I've had it up to here with women who run out when things get rough. Once, just once, I'd like to see a woman with the guts to see things through."

Startled, Gina stared at him. His face was lined with anger and pain, as if he'd reached some personal breaking point and couldn't take any more frustration. She suddenly had the absurd desire to reach out and comfort him, but she stifled it. A man like Colin Cassidy wouldn't understand empathy and compassion. He'd misinterpret it, probably putting it down to a desire for sex.

"All right, Mr. Cassidy," she said quietly. "I'll give it a shot."

He seemed to relax, but his face still mirrored distrust. "Good," he said shortly, then turned and strode toward the door. There he paused and looked back. "I'm sorry about being such a poor guest," he said, sounding defensive. "I guess I never learned the social amenities." With that, he pushed open the door and disappeared from the kitchen.

Slowly she began rinsing the dishes, a thoughtful look on her face. Again, she wondered what had happened in his life to make him this way. He was an enigma, and Gina loved to solve puzzles; they brought out the detective in her. Then she shook her head. The less she had to do with Colin Cassidy, the better. She would keep him on a last-name, professional-acquaintance basis and be done with him. A few months from now, when their taping was finished, she would probably say goodbye to him and never see him again. Tomorrow she would write out a check and drive him to the bank which was open Saturday mornings, and that would be that.

Happy that she had her life in control, she looked around the sparkling kitchen, sighed with satisfaction, snapped off the light and made her way to her bedroom. She saw the ribbon of light under the guest-room door and knew that Colin was still up. Maybe he was thumbing through one of the magazines she'd left for him or reading *Huckleberry Finn*. For some reason she couldn't fathom, that made her unreasonably happy. As she got ready for bed, she was surprised to find herself humming.

The next morning, Gina lay in bed and listened sleepily to the rain drumming on the roof, slamming against the windows, gurgling in the gutters. She snuggled deeper into the covers and turned on her stomach, wanting to drift back to sleep, then she roused herself from bed. She had her Saturday morning chores to do, so she couldn't afford to laze about in bed all day.

Still half asleep, she padded to the bathroom, the straps of her scanty black teddy falling off her shoulders, its neckline plunging dangerously low. Stifling a yawn and pushing back her cloud of black hair, she opened the door to the bathroom, then came to a complete stop. Opposite her, Colin had just opened the door that led from the guest room. He was clad only in skimpy Jockey shorts and was rubbing his chest and yawning gustily.

They both snapped wide awake at the same moment, then stood staring at each other. As she feasted her eyes on the magnificent male body before her, Gina felt a strange quivering begin in her midsection and spread like wildfire through the rest of her body. She didn't miss anything about him. She drank in the muscles that seemed sculpted from steel, the dark curly hair that covered his chest, the muscular arms and sinewy legs. As her gaze traveled back up, she couldn't help noticing him watching her. Instantly her cheeks turned to flame.

One corner of his mouth was turned up in amusement as his dark eyes met hers, then his gaze traveled lazily over her body, taking in the soft swell of her breasts, her slim hips beneath the high-cut legs of the teddy, and the long, silken length of her legs.

She instantly drew herself up, pulling her straps onto her shoulders while trying to raise her neckline without drawing his attention to it. She failed miserably. Colin's dark eyes lingered on her breasts, then rose to meet her wide-eyed gaze.

"You look good enough to have for breakfast," he drawled huskily.

She felt electric sparks radiate through her but forced herself to lift her chin defiantly, refusing to respond to his crude banter. "When you're finished with the bathroom, will you be kind enough to knock and let me know?" she asked stiffly.

"Do we have to be so formal?" Colin asked, grinning for the first time since she'd met him. "I could shave while you're showering. It'd be perfectly decent. I couldn't see through that shower curtain any more than I can see through your teddy. Probably less, as a matter of fact."

Appalled, she backed away, her hands at her neckline. "Please knock when you're finished, Mr. Cassidy," she said frostily, then slammed her door in his face and locked it. From behind it, she heard his low chuckle. Her cheeks burned. Shaking, she turned and made her way to the bed. Sinking down on it, she stared at the bathroom door.

It was good that he would be leaving today, she realized with alarm. Her body was still trembling in response to his presence. He was the most potently masculine man she'd seen in years, and at this proximity, her hormones were working overtime. Messages were humming through her nervous system, turning on little unseen switches and initiating automatic responses. Remembering the way his body had looked, she felt slightly giddy.

She pulled herself up short, appalled at her thoughts, and began to dress hurriedly, her hands still shaking. Somehow she would have to keep a lid on the cauldron that was burning inside her and get him out of this house. Once he was gone, she would be safe, but as long as he was here, she was in big trouble.

Four

———

Gina hurried through breakfast, doubly frightened. This morning Colin Cassidy was a changed man. The combination of a decent night's sleep and food seemed to alter him for the better, and she didn't like the change at all—he was even more attractive now, and he'd been plenty attractive before.

"Look, there's no need to hurry," he said at the end of the meal. "You said the bank will be open till noon."

She shook her head. "No, really. I'm sure you want to get going and find a place to stay. I'll bring you to my bank first, so you can cash my check, then—" She broke off, realizing his car was still in New Haven. "Oh, dear, how will you get your car?"

He shrugged. "I can always hitch a ride, I suppose."

"Hitch a ride in *this*?" she said, pointing to the driving rain that still pounded out of the heavens. She frowned, trying to come up with a reasonable alternative, but she couldn't think of anything except taking him there herself.

"I'll just have to drive you," she said irritably, wishing she could get him out of her hair. She didn't like all these electric feelings and yearnings that were zinging around her body.

"Look, I can hitch a ride," he said, sounding as exasperated as she.

"And I said I'll drive you!" she shot back.

They stood glaring at each other until she muttered a low curse and flung open the hall closet door and got her raincoat. After a second's thought, she pulled knee-high rubber boots over her shoes. From past experience, she knew the driveway could become almost impassable after a heavy rain. "Come on," she said testily. "We haven't got all day, you know."

"My God," he muttered, picking up his suitcase, "you *are* a cranky dame."

She slung him an angry look, then hurled open the door and dashed outside. What had been merely a sea of mud yesterday was now an ocean of the stuff. She stepped off the front porch into six inches of brown gunk. "Damn!" she muttered, then raised her right foot. It slurped and gurgled, lifting from the oozing glop with a bubbling *shlurppppp*. She took a tentative step and sank once again.

Slowly, with infinite care, Gina made her way toward the car, suctioning her feet one by one from the mud, listening to Colin's colorful curses behind her.

"Why didn't you tell me I'd need boots?" he demanded. "This is worse than a pigpen."

"How was I to know?" she called back. "It's never gotten this bad before."

"Great," he muttered darkly, drawing abreast of her.

She looked down and saw that his jeans legs were covered with mud. She couldn't even see his shoes. "I'm sorry," she murmured. "You are a mess, aren't you?"

"No worse than you," he snapped.

Glaring at him, she decided not even to try to be civil anymore. The man just didn't know how to react to a friendly overture.

When they reached the car, they threw themselves in with relief. The rain pelted down furiously on the roof and against the windows.

"So," Colin said with amiable irony, "this is what it's like living inside a snare drum."

Suddenly, Gina's lips quivered into a half smile. Valiantly she held back a giggle. "I think it's a monsoon," she said. "Maybe we got trapped in a time warp and got shifted to Malaysia or Singapore. Doesn't it rain like this over there?"

"Just drive, Longford," Colin said tiredly, staring down at his ruined shoes and jeans.

She started the car and put it in gear, but when she stepped on the gas, nothing happened. The engine whined and the tires spun, but they went nowhere. She accelerated harder, but the engine only whined louder while the wheels spun crazily.

"Oh, for crying out loud," Colin said, putting his head back and staring up at the car's ceiling.

"What's the matter with you?" Gina snapped, frowning as she floored the accelerator and the car impotently wheezed and roared, coughed and complained.

"We're stuck," Colin said with mock sweetness. "That's what's the matter with me."

"Stuck?" Gina stared at him, then slowly let up on the accelerator. She sat with her hands on the steering wheel, glumly looking out at the river of mud that had once been her driveway. "Of all the rotten luck," she said at last.

"Well, what do we do now, Longford?" Colin asked. "Walk the half mile to the main road or shall I get out and push us?"

The full impact of their situation finally hit her. Groaning, she leaned forward and rested her head against the steering wheel. They were really and truly stuck, in more ways than one. It might be days before the mud dried sufficiently so they could get the car out. "I'll call a tow truck," she said frantically. "They can pull us out."

"Then how will you get back in?" Colin asked practically. "Walk?"

She stared morosely at the mud and knew she would rather spend a week marooned with Colin Cassidy than face a half-mile hike from the main road in this mud.

"All right," she said finally, feeling as if her heart had dropped to her feet, "we'll stay put for now. I have plenty of food in the freezer. It can't rain much longer, and then the mud will dry and we'll get out of here." She sat gazing at the rain, then said bemusedly, "Of course, before that happens, we're liable to kill each other."

When Colin said nothing, she turned and looked at him. The expression on his face frightened her more than anything else during the past twenty-four hours. He was leaning against the door watching her with an expression of ironic amusement mingled with satisfaction. "I'm sure we could find other things to do than kill each other," he said in a low, seductive voice.

At that, Gina bolted. Throwing open the car door, she raced through the mud, squishing her way awkwardly back to the house, her heart throbbing, her pulses pounding. This was going to be impossible. She couldn't stay in the same house with that man another day and not break down. She couldn't! She was only human, dammit. She wasn't made of stone.

Reaching the porch, she put out a shaky hand and clutched the doorknob. She heard Colin approaching, then her eyes widened and she stared at the front door—her heart suddenly stopped.

He was whistling. Colin Cassidy, the surliest curmudgeon she'd ever had the displeasure of meeting, was actually whistling. She closed her eyes and rested her forehead against the front door. Oh, Lord, this was going to be worse than impossible. It was going to be a disaster. That rotten heel was already looking ahead and seeing them in bed together—she knew it.

Well, she would make damn sure he didn't get his way. If she had to bar her bedroom door and hole up like a hermit, she would resist his potent masculinity. It would be one thing if he were just a nice man she'd met—it had been a long time since she'd allowed herself any physical pleasure. But Colin was going to be working with her. That meant keeping their relationship strictly professional.

Before another minute elapsed, she was going to give him a message he couldn't misread. Straightening her shoulders, Gina kicked off her boots, opened the door and went in, then slammed the door in his face. Inside, she leaned back against it and closed her eyes. It was going to be a long weekend, she suspected. Long and arduous and extraordinarily trying.

Then, before she knew what was happening, the front door burst open and she was propelled halfway across the foyer. Torrents of rain rushed in on a gust of wind, and the rain-soaked, mud-spattered form of Colin Cassidy appeared.

"My *Lord*!" he said, brushing the rain off his denim jacket and shaking mud from his feet. "This is no monsoon. This is the biblical flood, come back to haunt us. All I want to know is, which one of us is Noah?''

Gina's eyes widened in horror as she watched him scatter rain and mud around her spotless foyer. "What are you *doing*?" she screeched. "Stop that this instant!"

He looked up at her, bemused. "Stop what? I'm only trying to dry off."

"Dry off out there!" she shouted, her hand shaking as she pointed toward the covered porch.

"Out *there*?" he shouted back. "That's like asking a person to swim in a dry pool."

"What a *horrible* analogy," she said, so angry she was shaking. "It isn't even in the least comparable."

"*I* don't give a damn about the analogy," he roared, staring at her as if she were crazy. "All I want is to get dry!"

"But look!" she said, pointing at the puddles at his feet, at the blobs of brown mud that dotted the lovely stone floor. "You've ruined my foyer!"

"Floors can be washed," he said, his voice rising right along with hers. "You are the most ridiculous dame I've ever stumbled across. Here I am, a human being, and you're more concerned with a damn pile of *rocks*!"

"They're not rocks, they're slate," she spat. "Vermont quarried slate. It's terribly expensive."

He glared at her, then took off his shoes and threw them defiantly on the floor. She stared, almost open-mouthed, but when he began to unbuckle his belt, her mouth really did open. On a scream.

"*What* do you think you're doing?" she demanded, her voice so high it risked breaking crystal.

"I'm getting undressed," he said. "What does it look like? Has it been so long since you've had a man in your life you don't even recognize one taking off his clothes?"

Stunned, she snapped her eyes up to his. "You boor," she said, her lip curled in contempt.

He unbuttoned his shirt and wadded it into a ball, then hurled it on the floor, nodding tightly all the while. "That's right. I'm a boor. I'm rude, contemptible and completely without manners. Now, *you*, on the other hand, are the epitome of charm. You make a person feel welcome and right at home."

He looked out at the driving rain and sea of mud and his face took on the look of desperation she'd imagined she would see on escaped convicts. He turned back to her, his eyes flashing fire. "I believe I'd do almost anything to get out of here, lady. I actually believe I'd descend to mayhem. That's why I'm going out there stripped down to my shorts, and I'm going to push that little car of yours up that half mile of mud, and *you* are going to help me!"

She blinked at him. "Help you?" she echoed, rallying. "Like hell I will. You can rot in the guest room before I'll put a foot out in that slime again to help you."

With that, she turned her back, but he reached out and grabbed her elbow and spun her around. Ebony eyes glared into hers. "Take off your clothes," he ordered ominously.

She simply stared. Finally she found her voice. "I beg your pardon?"

"You heard me. Take them off."

She didn't blink, didn't move a muscle. She simply looked him up and down, then laughed shortly, before she stalked off.

But not for long. "Lady," he said threateningly, "if you don't get behind the wheel of that car and steer while I push, I'll personally carry you out there and dump you behind it."

She folded her arms. "All right," she said, nodding curtly. "Carry me. I dare you. You put one finger on me, buster, and I'll ring your chimes so loud you'll think you're in the bell tower at Notre Dame.''

With his eyes fastened on hers, he nodded quickly then amazed her by stepping out of his pants. Her eyes widened, but she refused to acknowledge the two spots of hot color that blazed in her cheeks. Nor would she look down. Not for a million bucks and marriage to Prince Charming.

"For the last time," he said in an almost ordinary voice. "Are you going to take your clothes off?"

"I most certainly am not," she said stoutly, folding her arms protectively over her chest and lifting her chin disdainfully.

"Fine." He nodded shortly. Before she knew it, she was lifted by strong arms and clamped to a damp, bare chest. The odor of spicy male after-shave overcame her, along with the sensation of being devoured by ecstasy.

Strange thing about ecstasy—it was like tiny little electrical charges that crawled all over her, making her shiver with need, turning her bones to putty and her blood to lava. She swallowed thickly and told herself *not* to touch him, under any circumstance, then she promptly put her arms around his neck, staring fixedly at the darkish hint of beard under his freshly shaven cheeks.

Somersaults erupted in her stomach, which she vainly tried to ignore. It wasn't easy. Especially when she could so intimately feel him stirring into life against her. Panic overtook her. She struck at him weakly. "Put me down, you beast!"

"Oh, Gina," he said wearily, "just shut up." With that, he kicked open the front door and raced across the covered porch and down the steps. Then they were in it—assaulted by rain so devastatingly fierce it took their breath away. In a moment, they were both drenched.

"*Now* do you see why I asked you to take off your clothes?" he asked, his lips uncomfortably close to her ear.

She clung to him, trying to ignore his question along with his touch. But she'd never smelled anything as delicious as this rain-soaked man, and she'd never before felt this physically aroused.

Her fantasies were shortened when Colin flung open the car door and dumped her in the seat. She couldn't help it then, it just happened. She was at about eye level with his groin, and she simply stared, bemused.

"Not now, Gina, darling," Colin said dryly. "You'll have to wait until later, when we've had a lovely hot bath and are in bed together." He slammed the door and shouted for her to start the engine.

She sat there foolishly, cheeks burning, mortified. He'd read her mind, damn him! He'd seen right into her soul.

"Gina!" he roared from behind the car. "Start the damn engine. I'm drowning out here!"

"Serves you right, you bas—" She broke off, horrified by the language she'd been about to use. Well, it was Colin's fault, she reasoned. He was a boor and he was turning her into one. She looked around for her keys, then realized they were back on the table in the hall. A chuckle escaped her then escalated into outright laughter. She sat in the small car, feeling like a tuna trapped in a tin, her shoulders shaking as she laughed out loud.

Suddenly the door crashed open and Colin was there, bending to look in at her with a crazed look in his eyes. "Why are you laughing?" he asked, keeping his voice amazingly controlled. "What is so funny? Is there some joke I should know about? Perhaps you could share it with me."

She giggled softly, her hand on her mouth, as she looked at him out of the corner of her eye. "I can't start the car."

"You can't start the car."

"That's right. I can't start the car."

"Would you mind telling me why?" he asked. While he looked as if he might hit her, he sounded as courteous as a pastor at a christening.

"Because I don't have the keys. You see, this caveman swept me off my feet, clapped me over his shoulder and hauled me out here, but he didn't bother to think about taking along the car keys." She eyed him ironically. "Nor did he think about what he'd do when he got out on the road. You're nearly naked, you know, Colin."

He sighed wearily, then just stood there, letting the rain pelt off him. It ran in rivulets down his soaked chest, flattened the mat of dark hair, dripped off his chin, his nose, his lashes. Gina sat in the car, trying to hold back her laughter but not succeeding.

"Now if you'd like to go back for the keys and your clothing, Colin," she said in a perfectly reasonable voice, "I'd be more than happy to participate in this adorable little stunt you've dreamed up."

"I didn't clap you over my shoulder," he said quietly.

"What?" she asked, startled at the turn in the conversation.

"I said, I didn't clap you over my shoulder. I carried you, in my arms, the way a man carries a woman to bed."

She began to shake. Staring up at him, she felt the undercurrents of attraction flowing around them, felt the almost palpable throb of tension pulse in the air. Suddenly uneasy, she shifted in her seat and gripped the steering wheel. "We've gone this far," she said in a shaky voice. "We may as well continue."

"Just what I was thinking," he said in a low growl, then he dragged her from the car, and this time he *did* clap her over his shoulder, placing one strong hand on her backside.

"Colin!" she screeched. "What are you *doing*?"

He slammed the car door shut and traipsed back toward the house, mindless of the rain and mud. "I'm behaving like that caveman you think I am."

"But—" She held on for dear life, feeling her hands slide down his slippery back, trying to keep her eyes off his own beautifully developed derriere.

"But what, Gina?" Colin asked with resignation. "What's the problem now? Now I suppose you actually *want* me to push your car down to the road."

"Well, I—" He set her down on the porch with a thump that took her breath away. Dazed, she wiped her sodden hair out of her eyes and tried to catch her breath. "I thought that's what you wanted," she said, laughing nervously and backing toward the front door. "I mean, you made it clear you don't want to stay here. And *I* certainly don't want you here." She opened the door and gestured at the mess in the foyer. "Look at this mess. It's...it's..."

Colin closed the door and leaned back against it, eyeing her without speaking. Suddenly the room was absurdly quiet. After the din of the rain on the porch outside, the foyer sounded as hushed as an empty cathedral.

"It's what, Gina?" Colin asked, his voice sounding low and smoky.

She swallowed, rallying her defenses. "It's disgusting," she said weakly. "Clothing scattered around, and mud all over the place, and puddles...." She pushed back a strand of wet hair and blinked rain out of her eyes. "Why, it'll take me all day just to get the hall cleaned up, and by then you'll have ruined the bathroom." She glanced at him uneasily then quickly looked away.

"No," she said loudly, resolutely. "You can't stay here. That's final. I'll write you a check and you can walk down to the main road and hitch a ride." She scrambled in her pocketbook, searching wildly for her checkbook. "That's the only solution. There's just no other way. I'll just write the check and you can dress and get out of here. Don't even think about staying another moment. It won't work, Colin. That's final."

Then he sneezed.

Slowly she lifted her eyes and stared at him. He was soaking wet, absolutely drenched, from the top of his head to the tips of his toes. She narrowed her eyes. Had that sneeze been a ploy? Had he sneezed to get sympathy and sneak behind her defenses? She hardened her heart, determined to get him out of there, then he sneezed again, and her heart melted.

"Oh, God," she said softly, "you're catching a cold."

"A cold, like hell," he said sourly. "I'm catching pneumonia. I'll probably die halfway up your driveway. Ten days from now, when the mud dries, you'll find me, and *then* you'll be sorry."

"Oh, Colin," she whispered, hurrying into the living room and finding her softest angora throw. "Here," she said, rushing back and tucking it around his shoulders. "This will warm you a little. I'll run a nice hot bath for you and make tea and I'll build a fire and turn the heat up and you'll be fine. You'll see."

In response, he sneezed again, eyeing her crankily. "I'm warning you, I'm a terrible patient."

"I know," she said soothingly, guiding him toward the guest room, "all men are. You're all such babies when you get the least little germ."

"I don't like women fussing around me, either," he growled, letting her lead him toward the bedroom. "I want to be left alone. I want to throw my tissues on the floor and leave my empty coffee cups lying around, and I want to watch television twenty-four hours a day, preferably the Three Stooges.''

The Three Stooges? Tissues littering the floor? Coffee cups with green mold clinging to them? She felt her heart begin to harden again. Fastidiously she lifted her hand and stepped back.

He eyed her knowingly. "Well, Longford, what'll it be? Me here recuperating from a cold, making your life hell, or out there catching pneumonia and dying? Would it bother you if my soul were on your conscience?"

She folded her arms and tapped her toe. "You lowlife," she said accusingly. "I'm almost tempted to let you leave. You're playing this for all it's worth, tugging at my heartstrings, appealing to the humanitarian in me."

He shook his head, shivering beneath the angora throw. "Uh-uh," he said, then sneezed. "A dame like you doesn't have a heart in the first place, much less heartstrings, and in the second place, you wouldn't recognize a humanitarian impulse if it reached out and bit you."

That did it. He'd effectively doused every flame of ardor that had threatened to overcome her. She was as cold as the Arctic now, and about as willing to go to bed with him as with a grizzly.

"Since you think I'm heartless, Mr. Cassidy," she said gently, "you can just take care of yourself. You know where the towels are. I'd recommend a nice hot bath, then a couple of days of bed rest. No tissues on the floor—they spread germs. No empty coffee cups sitting around, for the same reason. And no television, period. Is that clear?"

"You want to kill me," he accused.

She eyed him triumphantly. "It's certainly crossed my mind," she said airily, then abruptly walked away.

Five

"Longford!"

Colin's bellow reverberated through the small cottage, reaching Gina as she sipped tea in the kitchen. Her lips narrowed threateningly as she made her way toward the guest room. Damn the man—if he didn't stop annoying her with his foolish demands every two seconds, she would bean him with a skillet and be done with him forever.

"What is it now?" she demanded, throwing open the door to the guest room. The sight that greeted her took her breath away. A half-dozen magazines were scattered over the floor, wadded-up tissues surrounded the bed, and the coverlet on her precious pencil-post antique bed had been kicked off and lay haphazardly on the floor. At the sight of the mess, her eyes ignited.

"How do you *do* it?" she screeched, running around gathering tissues and stuffing them in a wastebasket.

"You're worse than a child! My nephew isn't this destructive and he's only seven!"

"Oh, Longford," Colin said lazily, "button it up, will you? Just give a guy a break." He picked up the half-empty teacup and held it out. "This stuff is going to kill me. What I need is a pint of Jack Daniel's. Think you can scare one up for me?"

"Do you have a death wish?" she asked, staring at him bemusedly. "You're filled with cold medication. If you drank even a little liquor, you'd probably shuffle off this mortal coil and I'd be stuck with the funeral bill." She snorted. "Not that anyone would come to *your* funeral. We could shove you in one of those pauper's graves and be done with it. I'll bet not a soul on earth would miss you."

"No, but at least I'd have a passel of them waiting for me in hell when I got there," he said darkly, then sneezed.

For no logical reason his sneezing melted her heart. She couldn't be angry at him when the evidence of his misery was so patently obvious. "Oh, Colin," she said softly, tucking the coverlet around his shoulders and smoothing a hand over his hot brow. "You're sick, Colin. I think you've got a fever. You've got to take care of yourself."

He yanked his head away irritably. "Like hell. I need some Jack Daniel's, dammit. That'll fix me up fine."

"Colin," she said severely, "you've got to let me take your temperature."

"Oh, sure," he said sarcastically. "Anything to get me to turn over and..."

"Colin!" Shocked, she could only stare down at him, her cheeks aflame with embarrassment. "I'd use an oral thermometer, Mr. Cassidy," she said primly. "I assure you, I have no desire to...to..."

"See my bum?"

She shuddered. He was totally crude. Why had she let him into her house?

"You almost saw it this morning," he said, coughing and grinning at the same time. "I kinda got the idea you wanted to see more."

She rolled her eyes as she smoothed the sheets over his naked chest. "I wish you wore undershirts or pajamas," she fretted. "You need to cover up. You really *are* going to catch pneumonia if you don't watch out."

He ran a hand up her bare arm. "Climb in beside me, then," he suggested drowsily. "Keep me warm."

She drew in a quick breath and removed her arm from his grasp. "You're delirious."

"Like hell. I'm a red-blooded male."

She arched a wry brow. "Right now, Mr. Cassidy, you're in no condition to act on your impulse. Just lie back and try to get some rest. I'll make you more tea."

"No more tea," he said crankily. "I hate the stuff."

"It's good for you."

"Like hell it is. It's probably sapping my strength. You've probably put saltpeter in it, like they do in the army. I tell you, what I need is some booze."

She folded her arms and looked down at him as if he were a recalcitrant bum. "Mr. Cassidy, why is it that you think only of sex and liquor?"

"Because they're the only two things that make life worthwhile. Bring me a bottle of Jack Daniel's and climb into bed with me, and I guarantee you I'll be well in a day."

"Dream on, Cassidy."

"Okay," he said. "Have it your way, but I'm warning you—I'll get sicker."

"I can handle you."

He eyed her in exasperation. "Longford, you couldn't handle me if you had written instructions and I guided you every step of the way."

"Why don't we just try it?" she suggested cheerfully. "Write down the instructions and let's see how I do."

Irritably he waved away her words. "No need to write them down. They're simple: take your clothes off, get in bed and let nature take its course. The only trouble is, you're not woman enough to know even the first thing about how nature takes its course."

"You reduce everything to the lowest common element, don't you, Cassidy?" she asked coldly. "You have the lurid ability to turn something beautiful like making love into something disgusting. I really pity you, Cassidy. I truly do." With that, she turned toward the door.

"I pity you more, Longford," he shouted after her. "It's your loss. I'm hell on wheels in bed."

"In your condition?" she asked wryly. "Uh-uh, Cassidy, I sincerely doubt it."

She closed the door softly then heard a rolled-up magazine hit the door a second later. Suppressing a grin at this sign of his anger, she returned to her tea in the kitchen.

Four hours later, it hit her that he hadn't called out to her, hadn't made any of his ridiculous demands, hadn't, in fact, bothered her once since she'd left him earlier. She tiptoed down the hall and inched open the guest-room door.

He was sleeping, but the covers were thrown off. At the sight of his body, a sudden wave of heat rippled through her. His chest rose and fell in uneasy breathing, and she couldn't help noticing the rest of him that was exposed to view. His body was magnificent, and it took all her effort not to let it affect her.

Tiptoeing across the room, she reached the side of his bed and then hesitated. She'd intended to pull the covers up and smooth them over him, but she saw that he was bathed in sweat and shivering at the same time.

Suddenly alarmed, she pulled the sheets and coverlet up then dashed into the bathroom for supplies. She would have to dry him off and keep him warm or he really *would* catch pneumonia. A sudden chill went through her. Even in these modern times, pneumonia wasn't anything to laugh at. What if he needed antibiotics? How would she get medicine to him if her driveway were impassable?

She grabbed a set of sheets, a stack of towels and three blankets and rushed back to the bedroom. She began drying the sweat from his face, neck and shoulders. He groaned and moved restlessly, trying to push her away.

"It's all right, Colin," she whispered softly. "I'm here, you're going to be fine."

For some reason, her words seemed to work and he relaxed and let her dry his body. Then she rolled him to one side of the bed and quickly stripped off the soaked bottom sheet, put a new sheet on and rolled him to the other side, completing her work in mere minutes, then added a new top sheet and three blankets.

"Sally?"

His raspy voice made her pause. She stared at him, inexplicably hurt that he'd called out for another woman, someone named Sally. Hadn't that been the name of the woman who'd moved out on him? Yes, Sally was the daughter of his former publisher in Albuquerque.

Gina sat down on the edge of the bed and smoothed her hand over his fiery brow. "No, Colin," she said soothingly, "it's not Sally. It's Gina."

He frowned and began to struggle. Valiantly she held him down until he quieted, then she continued stroking his brow.

"It's all right, Colin," she said in a low, soothing voice. "I'm here. You're not alone. You're going to be all right, Colin. I won't leave you."

Suddenly his face changed. The pain, fatigue and fear vanished, and he seemed almost to smile. In turn, his half smile worked wonders on Gina, filling her with an incredible sense of peace and accomplishment, as if she'd done something truly worthwhile. Maybe this was how nurses and doctors felt when they labored over a difficult case in the hospital.

She started to get up, but he reached out and took her hand in a surprisingly strong grip. "You said you'd stay," he grumbled. He opened his eyes and stared up at her, but she realized he didn't recognize her even though he continued to hold her hand tightly.

She sat down on the bed again. "That's right, Colin," she murmured softly. "I won't leave. I'll stay."

"You can't leave," he went on, as if he hadn't heard her. "You're always walking out. All the time. All of you. You never stay. None of you. A man can't depend on any of you. A man needs a woman he can depend on."

Troubled, Gina stared down at the anguish in Colin's face then reached out and stroked his forehead. "Shhh," she whispered comfortingly, "it's all right, Colin, darling. I'm here. I won't leave you. You can depend on me. Go to sleep, sweetheart."

His face changed again, the anguish disappearing and an almost angelic expression of trust sweeping over it. He closed his eyes and his lips curved in a blissful smile. Watching him, Gina swallowed thickly, feeling compassion well up within her. She couldn't leave now. Something told her he really needed her. He'd obviously been let down by women before, and now he needed a woman he could trust.

Biting her lip, Gina looked around the room. Perhaps she could pull a chair next to the bed and sit and hold his hand. Then she felt him shiver. Concerned, she bent down and saw that he was shaking with chills. She put out a hand and felt his forehead. It was burning up, yet he shivered as if he were exposed to Arctic air.

Truly frightened, she realized she had to do something quickly or he really might get very ill. Calling a doctor might have been a good idea, but who in their right mind would come out in this weather? She'd read once that a human's body heat was the most warming thing on earth. She made her decision quickly. Standing up, she hurriedly took off all her clothing and climbed under the covers and nestled up to him. The sudden contact with his fiery skin unnerved her at first, then she forgot the exquisite sensual pleasure and concentrated on his condition. He was ill and might get worse before he got better. Then a dark thought crossed her mind. Maybe he wouldn't get better at all.

Reaching out, she put her arms around him and snuggled against him, resting her head on his chest and nestling as close to him as possible. For a long time she lay holding him, feeling his large, strong body racked by shivers even as it radiated fiery heat. For what seemed like hours, she lay staring into the darkness, worry gnawing at her breast until finally she couldn't fight her own weariness. Slowly her lashes lowered. Valiantly she tried to open her eyes, only to ultimately fail.

She yawned sleepily and wriggled closer to Colin, then smiled when his strong arm went around her in his sleep, pulling her closer. She rested a slim hand on his muscular chest and dimly registered the strong, regular beat of his heart, then she slid into sleep, a soft smile curving her lips, her body relaxed, feeling more comfortable than she had in years....

* * *

She was dreaming. A man's strong hand was on her breast, and his thumb was brushing softly back and forth across her aroused nipple. She smiled beatifically and stretched like a cat, arching her back and yawning lustily, then moaning softly as the large, warm hand cupped her breast and massaged it gently.

Lord, what a wonderful dream! She rolled onto her back and drifted into it further, allowing the delightful sensations to shiver over her body as the hand worked its sensual magic. She slid deeper into sleep, only to rouse slightly when his palm moved lightly down her midriff and began to lovingly stroke the soft swell of her tummy.

A delighted smile broke over her face. She rolled onto her side and threw her leg over the man's body, arching her body closer to his and gasping in pleasure when his hand slid between her legs.

"Mmm," she crooned, smiling in her sleep. "Yes. There."

"Right there?" the man's low voice asked.

"Mmm," she said, smiling dreamily.

Pleasure cascaded over her in rivers, drowning her in exquisite ecstasy. She moaned again and pushed her abdomen toward the man and was rewarded with the feel of his arousal throbbing against her stomach. She groaned out loud and rolled onto her back, putting her arms around the man as he rolled with her. She was ready. She'd never been more ready to make love in her entire life.

Then she opened her eyes.

"Good morning," Colin said from atop her.

Frozen midway between ecstasy and hell, she stared into his dark eyes. "Oh God," she moaned, "it's not a dream."

"No," he said amiably, "but it sure feels like one, doesn't it?"

She was suddenly vividly aware of the intimacy of their position. Blood rushed into her cheeks as cold panic entered her breast. "Get off of me," she said shakily.

"You wanted me on you just a minute ago."

"A minute ago, I thought this was a dream."

"So close your eyes again and let's pretend, darlin'," he drawled.

"Get off," she commanded from between gritted teeth. If the truth be known, she didn't know which she was fighting more—him or her own impulses.

He sighed regretfully but nevertheless rolled off her, then had the audacity to grin at her as if they'd slept together for years. "Sure felt good, didn't it?"

Shaking, she pulled up a blanket and covered her breasts. "I think you're totally disgusting," she said with a trembling voice.

"Oh, baloney," he said good-naturedly. "Any woman who moans and cuddles like you do doesn't think I'm disgusting. You like it, Gina Longford, admit it. Sex is like food to you, and I've got a hunch you've been on a starvation diet for way too long. Looks like it's lucky for both of us I happened into your life."

"Get one thing straight, buddy," she said, climbing out of bed while holding the blanket up to her. "You're not *in* my life, in any way, shape or form, except as cohost of a television program. I got into bed with you last night because you were bathed in sweat and shivering with cold and I was terrified I was going to end up with a corpse on my hands." She gestured back and forth between them and the bed. "This was strictly humanitarian, Cassidy, nothing else. Is that understood? You took advantage of me. I was *sleeping*, dammit! I'm not responsible for what I do in my sleep."

"Neither am I," he said reasonably. "You're making me out to be the bad guy in this and I'm just as innocent as you.

I was sleeping, too. I felt this warm, soft, sexy body next to mine and I began to respond. It was instinctive, Gina, nothing else. Don't blame me for doing what comes naturally."

"But you woke up before I did," she accused.

"A half a second, maybe," he admitted.

She peered at him sideways, as if from that angle she could better detect a lie. "I don't believe you."

He shrugged. "Believe what you want. Knowing you, I couldn't convince you if I were an angel sent from heaven."

"An angel sent from heaven wouldn't have done what you were doing."

"No?" Colin grinned. "I'll bet that's what they do all the time up in heaven."

She stiffened. "That's utter blasphemy!"

"Why should it be? I've got just as much right to my version of heaven as you do. I'll bet you think they sit around up there all day playing the harp or something."

She tossed her head at him. Honestly, the man was sick with fever. He'd obviously lost touch with reality. "You are still a very sick man, Mr. Cassidy. I'd suggest you cover up and let me bring you some breakfast."

"Don't bring any tea," he warned.

She raised her chin. "Tea is what you'll get, and I don't want to hear another word about it. You're darned lucky to be alive. When I came in here yesterday, you were on the verge of pneumonia. Now lie there and stop ordering me around. I give the orders around here, and you take them. Is that clear?"

He propped his head on his arms and smiled. "Aye-aye, Major."

She gathered her blanket more securely around her and shuffled toward the bathroom. "I have to shower and get dressed," she said stiffly, "then I'll bring you your breakfast."

She closed the bathroom door behind her and sighed with relief. She was still shaking, but luckily she'd escaped with some of her dignity intact. She let the blanket fall to the floor and turned on the shower, made sure the water was good and hot, then climbed in and pulled the curtain shut. A moment later the bathroom door opened.

She froze, wide-eyed. "Colin?"

"Yup."

"What are you doing in here?"

"I *am* human, Gina," he said. "I'm doing what any other human would do who hasn't done it in over twelve hours."

Her face went red. She crossed her arms over her body and huddled in a corner of the tub, as if she were afraid he'd tear back the shower curtain and ravish her.

She heard the toilet flush, then the sound of water splashing in the basin. Craning her head to one side, she could barely discern the sound of Cassidy gargling from beyond the spray of her shower. "Do you *have* to brush your teeth now?" she demanded indignantly.

"Yesh," he said, sounding as if he had a mouthful of mush.

She considered that, then shrugged. Oh well, no sense fighting it. She waited for a moment until she heard the door close then dared to peer from behind the shower curtain. The bathroom was once again empty. She was alone—and safe.

Letting out a deep breath, she began to lather herself with soap, wondering how in heaven's name she would face Colin

Cassidy after what had just transpired between them. If things had been bad yesterday, they were twenty times worse today.

Yesterday, after all, Colin had only suspected she was attracted to him. Today, he knew she was.

Six

So tell me about this Sally," Gina suggested later that afternoon. Colin was feeling well enough to sit up, so they were sharing a light snack of tea and toast in the kitchen. Outside, the rain still hammered against the windows, pounded on the roof and rushed pell-mell down the gutters, filling the world with foot-deep puddles.

"There's nothing to tell," Colin muttered, making a nasty face at his cup of tea.

"Liar," Gina said lightly. "You called out for her yesterday."

"I did not!" Colin said, jerking his head up to stare at Gina in genuine amazement.

"You most certainly did," Gina gloated. "As a matter of fact, you said lots of things in your delirium yesterday." She liked it that she knew more about Colin's behavior than he did; it gave her a sense of mastery over this ticklish situation.

"What did I say?" Colin asked uneasily.

Colin's obvious discomfort further heightened Gina's sense of control. She propped her elbows smugly on the table and plopped her chin on her folded hands. "Oh, you rambled on and on about how women can't be trusted, that we all run away, that sort of thing. Lots of generals and no real specifics, except for Sally. You really *did* call out for her."

Colin idly stirred his tea, his head cocked to the side as he studied Gina. "Your behavior is so typical of a woman," he said finally. "You don't know the meaning of the word tact. Instead of pretending that nothing happened, you have to meddle and pry and snoop into every corner that doesn't concern you, and the whole time you sit there looking as if you have every right in the world to know these things that aren't your business in the least."

At that, Gina sat up straight, her earlier smugness gone. "I wasn't prying," she said stiffly. "I was merely attempting to make civil conversation, something *you* haven't the least understanding of or ability to do." She tossed her head, sending her hair flying around her shoulders. "Of course, I suppose I shouldn't expect social graces from a *man*," she went on, spreading butter thickly on her toast. "None of you understands the social graces in the least. You think small talk is silly, while we women know it's utterly necessary." Gina shrugged airily, bit hungrily into her toast and swallowed. "Small talk is the oil that greases a relationship, the lace that binds men and women together, the cement that keeps a relationship from crumbling apart."

"What would you know about man-woman relationships?" Colin asked grumpily. "You've got one failed marriage to show for all that smart airy-fairy talk of yours."

Stricken by his words, Gina could only stare at Colin. Then she rallied. "Well, at least *I* made an *attempt*," she snapped. "You were probably too cowed by the idea of making a commitment to a woman to even try marriage." She snorted derisively. "Either that, or every woman you ever asked knew better than to accept."

"I never asked anyone," he barked. "*I* knew better."

"Ha! I knew it!" Gina gloated. "You haven't got the guts. You're the kind who wants all the perks of marriage and none of the responsibilities."

"The perks?" he asked, his voice rising in amazement. "You mean to tell me there *are* some?"

Gina began to enumerate them on her fingers: "Companionship, sharing life's burdens as well as joys, the opportunity to build a life together, to travel together, to nestle up on cold nights and know that the person you're with won't desert you." She tossed her hair back knowingly. "And, of course, number one on the male's hit parade: sex, every night and every morning, and three or four times on weekends if the mood strikes you."

"I can get all that without marriage," Colin snarled. "And, believe me, the sex is better when there's no commitment. The minute a woman gets a ring on her finger, she crosses her legs and doles out sex as if it's the most precious commodity in the world, not to mention the rarest."

"How would you know?" she shot back. "You've never even been married."

"I've got friends," he said, his voice rising along with hers. "I've heard the horror stories about the headaches every night that you women suddenly develop after the marriage ceremony is over."

"*I* never had headaches," Gina asserted hotly, then put a hand to her mouth, embarrassed at what she'd just inadvertently admitted.

Slowly the atmosphere in the kitchen changed. Colin sat and stared at her, his dark eyes taking on a curious gleam.

He stroked his lower lip thoughtfully, drawing Gina's attention to it.

She sucked in her breath painfully. It was a beautiful lower lip—full, curved and sensual. She had a sudden premonition of what it would be like to kiss him, to feel his lips moving against hers, to feel his hands unbuttoning and unzipping, sliding her clothes off and gliding his strong hands over her skin.

She swallowed painfully, unable to look him in the eye. Suddenly the room was too quiet and too small. She felt as if she and Colin were crowded into a tiny elevator that was stuck between floors. There seemed no way out, no way past his dark, knowing eyes.

"These past few years must have been difficult for you, then," Colin said in a low voice.

She glanced at him and saw that his lips were curved in a curiously knowledgeable smile. "Why do you say that?" she asked, feeling strangled.

"You obviously enjoyed the sex in your marriage, if nothing else. It must be difficult living a celibate life."

She rubbed the back of her neck with a shaking hand and fiddled nervously with an errant curl. "I've managed. Besides, my life isn't exactly celibate," she said, mortified to find that her voice was shaking as much as her hands.

"Really?" He made the question seem almost like a challenge, as if he didn't believe her for a moment.

She shifted uncomfortably in her chair. "I keep busy. Sex isn't everything, you know. There are plenty of other compensations."

"Such as?"

She sat and tried to think of one. Just one. Even a small compensation would do, but her mind was blank. Fretfully she rubbed her hands together. "Well," she said, laughing nervously, "there's my job. I mean, I love my work, and it keeps me very busy."

"How do you deal with the love scenes on screen when you're doing a review?" Colin asked idly.

She felt two red patches begin to glow in her cheeks. "They don't bother me," she lied. "It's like being a gynecologist, I assume. After a while, he doesn't see women as women. They're just patients."

"So when you see two actors up on the screen and they're really, um—involved, you don't feel anything?"

"Well..." Gina cleared her throat and brushed away some toast crumbs. "Well, of course, as a *critic* I feel something. I mean, the response evoked *is* one way of evaluating a scene's effectiveness, after all."

"So you get turned on by some of the movies you review, then."

"No!" she snapped, then shook her head in bewilderment. "Well, not *turned on*, not in so many words. It's more like aesthetic appreciation. I mean, you wouldn't stand in front of a painting by Goya and get 'turned on,' now, would you?" She rubbed her hands together uneasily, trying to think of a way to end this conversation. Instead, with every word, she seemed to dig herself into a deeper hole. "I mean, it's the critic's job to evaluate a scene's effectiveness, among other things, but—"

She lifted her wide eyes to Colin and saw that he was sitting back with his arms folded across his muscular chest, a satisfied grin on his face. "Don't feel so bad, Gina. I get turned on, too," he murmured softly.

Somehow, his confession made things even more personal. She became even more aware of his presence, of the way his freshly shaven skin looked, of the dark hair that escaped from his open shirt collar, the curve of his lips, the masculine thrust of his shoulders beneath his snugly fitted denim shirt.

She felt a strange tightening of her breasts, as if her nipples were puckering under the pressure of seeking lips and a probing tongue. A sudden sense of urgency seemed to permeate the air and invade her body, and she felt a delicious sense of temptation flow through her.

She hadn't felt this way in years, hadn't felt the desire to kiss a man, to hold him and be held, to feel his bare, hair-roughened skin, inhale his scent, hear his whispered love-words as his breath played over her ear and neck. There was something deliciously illicit about all this, something dangerously provocative. She felt as if she were engaged in a battle between the part of her that said no and the part that wanted to say yes.

And, oh, it was exciting! Somehow life became larger. Words meant more. Gestures became more telling. Little signs that might have earlier escaped one's notice became enchanting signposts that pointed the way to ecstasy.

Gina sat and stared at Colin and realized what this was all about—ecstasy. You could have the most wonderful job in the world, the cutest, most adorable home, the nicest car, the best clothes, the biggest paycheck, but if you didn't have a man to hold you, the rest of that went a little flat. The plain fact was, the world didn't stand still over fat paychecks and new furniture, she didn't find her heart hammering deliciously over fast cars, didn't lose her breath when a designer declared her new dress the smartest in Connecticut.

Only a man could have that effect on her. A man, with a wonderful body, smooth skin that felt like satin under a woman's gentle hands, muscular arms and shoulders, sinewy thighs and rock-hard calves, an abdomen that rippled with muscles, lips that coaxed reluctant kisses, a tongue that seduced a woman by licking and sucking until she thought she would lose her mind from the rapture of it all....

Gina lowered her gaze to the tabletop but didn't see a thing. Instead, she envisioned herself with Colin, in bed, naked. She saw their limbs entwined, saw his lips on her breasts, his hands moving in slow motion over her body, felt the delicious tremor his kisses would produce. She remembered with vivid clarity the way he'd slid his hand between her legs that very morning. The actual physical sensations returned, rippling through her, turning her to buttery softness, filling her with a need such as she hadn't felt in years.

A sense of urgency permeated her body. She seemed heavier suddenly, as if she were weighed down by physical sensations. Instinctively she knew all she had to do was lift her head and look at Colin and it would happen. He would stand up and come around the table and take her in his arms. He would carry her to the bedroom and undress her and....

Taking a shaky breath, Gina stood up so quickly that her chair overturned. Ignoring it, she nervously began to gather the dishes, clattering the silverware and clinking the teacups together, until finally Colin stood up, too.

"Nervous, Gina?" he asked mildly.

"Not in the least," she said cheerfully. "Why do you ask?"

"Your chair is lying on the floor, overturned. You almost broke two teacups and a saucer. You dropped a knife and two spoons." He shrugged. "I guess I just thought something might have happened to make you a little uneasy."

"Me? Uneasy?" She laughed brightly and promptly stumbled on the overturned chair, sending her into a zany, slapstick dance toward the kitchen sink as she balanced the tower of dishes that wobbled unsteadily in her hands.

"Let me help," Colin said, appearing as if by magic at her side.

"No!"

But it was too late. He was there, next to her, his aftershave scenting the air, his body blocking out the rest of the world. He took the stack of dishes from her and suddenly the world righted itself. She took a deep breath and sank against the kitchen counter, watching as he safely deposited the dishes in the sink. But she was more aware of his size and the shape of his body, of the hard muscles, the dark hair, the musky smell that emanated from the depths of his being.

Then she remembered that he was recovering from sickness. "Here," she said, quickly reaching out. "Let me do that."

Their hands touched and the world spun crazily out of control. She jumped back, and at the same time a teacup smashed to the floor, scattering in all directions. Her hand flew to her mouth. "Oh!"

Colin went down on one knee and began gathering up the pieces. "Was it very important to you?" he asked, pausing in his work to look up at her.

She stared down at him, unable to look away from his eyes. They were the darkest eyes she'd ever seen, but she noticed for the first time that his pupils sparkled, as if they were gilded by gold flakes, as if pieces of the sun had broken off and landed there.

"Was it very important to you?" he repeated, his eyes holding hers.

"Important?" She stared at him, bemused by his question. What in heaven's name was he talking about? "Was what important?"

"The teacup."

"Oh." She stared into his eyes then dragged her gaze to the shattered cup. "Oh, no. It's just a silly cup. I've got a dozen others like it." She stared at the pieces some more, as if seeing them for the first time. "Well, actually, it's Bavarian china and terribly expensive, but..." She shrugged. "Easy come, easy go."

"With my first paycheck, I'll buy you a new one to replace it."

She shook her head, smiling. "Please don't. It was my fault. My fingers were shaking and I—" She broke off, blushing furiously.

Slowly Colin stood up. "Your fingers were shaking?"

She couldn't reply, was struck dumb. She could only stand and stare into his eyes, feeling the relentless tug of attraction pulling her toward him.

"Why were your fingers shaking?" he persisted, his voice low, almost slumberous.

"I..." She backed away, then stopped. "I don't know," she said, shrugging.

"You must be nervous."

She shook her head. "I have nothing to be nervous about."

"Then perhaps you're excited?"

"I have nothing to be excited about." Her voice shook as she spoke. She wanted to kick herself.

"Maybe it's my presence," Colin suggested. "Maybe it's unnerving to have a man in your virginal house."

She blinked but didn't look away. "My house isn't virginal."

"Monastic, then."

Silence seemed to fill the room, but try as she might, she couldn't think of a reply. She could only stand and stare into his eyes, feeling herself being sucked nearer and nearer to the edge of what felt like a dark whirlpool.

"That's it, isn't it, Gina Longford?" he asked, his voice hypnotically low. "It's my presence. I unnerve you. I make you remember things you've tried too long to forget."

She backed away a step. "What sort of things?" she asked, trying to sound puzzled.

"The presence of a man in your home. The sound of a man's voice, his scent in the bathroom, his clothes on the floor, his laughter...."

She backed away another step. "I haven't missed any of those things," she asserted weakly.

"No? Well, then, perhaps I misjudged you or did you an injustice, Gina. Perhaps what you've missed is the feel of a man in your arms, the feel of his lips on yours, of his hands on your body. You liked it this morning well enough. You moaned and arched your back like a satisfied cat. You even told me where you liked me to touch you."

She took an uneven breath and tried to look away, to marshal her forces, but she had little strength left to fight the potent attraction that exploded around them. His words acted like a match on kerosene. What had been merely the promise of a bonfire was now threatening to rage out of control.

"You have no right to say those things," she said in a low, shaky voice. "You're no gentleman, Mr. Cassidy."

"That's right," he agreed affably. "No more than you're a lady. We both want the same thing, Gina. I'm just more honest than you."

"And what is it we both supposedly want, Mr. Cassidy?" she asked coolly, happy she was able to control the quiver in her voice.

His dark eyes glinted as his gaze flickered up and down her body. "Why, each other, of course," he said, with a hint of a smile. "We want each other, Gina Longford, the way a man and a woman always want each other—in bed."

Now that it was said, she felt as if she might collapse. Hot currents of desire shot through her body, but she valiantly tried to fight them. She turned her back and carefully began to stack the dishes in the dishwasher.

"I'm sorry, Mr. Cassidy, but you're mistaken. Perhaps your fever has returned. Or perhaps you've merely misread me. I'm not interested in having an affair with you, no matter how discreet." She closed the dishwasher door and dried her hands on a crisp linen towel. "And I'd appreciate it if you'd drop the subject. I don't ever want to discuss it again. Is that clear?" She turned to face him, still trembling but knowing she had to somehow prove she meant what she said.

"One thing is clear, Gina Longford—you're scared to death of me. You're so scared you're shaking. And I don't mean you think that I'll hurt you in any way. I don't mean to imply that you're afraid you've invited some criminal into your home. You're scared of me as a man. You know if we ever went to bed together, you'd be lost. I'm exactly what you need and you know it, and that knowledge scares the hell out of you."

Before she could think, she raised her hand to slap him. He merely stood and smiled at her, his eyes knowing, taunting, filled with derision as he reached out and caught her hand, then held it in a viselike grip.

"Ah-ah," he taunted softly. "Temper, temper."

She wrenched her hand from his and turned on her heel. "Stay out of my way, Cassidy," she said coldly. "We may be stuck here, but we don't have to associate with each other. I don't want to hear you and I don't want to see you. Is that clear? One peep out of you and I'll throw you out in that monsoon, and if you get pneumonia, I'll personally dig your grave."

"Tough talk, Gina," he said softly.

She turned at the door and looked back at him. She was still trembling, but she was far enough away from him to feel safe. "I mean it, Cassidy. Every word."

He shook his head. "No, you don't, Gina," he said quietly. "You don't mean a word of it. But I'll give you time. I'll grant it's a shock for something like this to happen so quickly, but it has, Gina, and you've got to face it. The tension's so thick between us, we could cut it with a knife. I could lock myself in that guest room of yours, but I guarantee you, sooner or later, you'd unlock that door and crawl into bed with me. That's just the way it is between us. Face it, lady."

She heard his words with a sick heart. Tears sprang into her eyes. If only it were that simple. If only life were like men painted it. "No," she whispered brokenly, "I hate what you just said—I hate everything it stands for. You make it sound like animal lust, like something dirty." She straightened, and her voice grew stronger, as if somewhere deep inside she'd somehow found those reserves she'd needed to withstand his attraction.

"You may be content with sex, Colin Cassidy, but I'm not. When I go to bed with a man, I go because I love him. I go because I can't bear to be apart from him, because we complete each other. You and I could never have that, Cassidy, never in a million years. You want an amiable romp in the hay with no strings attached, and I want a companion for life."

She stared at him with eyes filled with pain. "And you know what's sad, Cassidy?" she asked softly. "In one way, you're right. We *do* want each other. The physical part is all there, just ready to be plucked, as ripe as peaches on a tree. It's the other part that's missing between us, the part with the heart and the soul and the magic. And I won't settle for anything less.''

Turning, she walked out of the kitchen. She was glad she knew the way to her room, for her eyes were clouded with tears.

Seven

Living with Cassidy after that was a little like living in a mine field, Gina decided. Even one false move could prove disastrous: she would end up in bed with him or he would end up camped out on her porch for the duration of the rain.

And it continued to rain, as if God had forgotten the Flood and had arranged this deluge strictly for the purpose of bringing these two wholly unsuitable companions together as mates.

Gina cleaned house diligently and Colin messed it up as quickly as she cleaned it. They were at an uneasy standoff, ready to snarl at each other or fall into each other's arms. Neither seemed sure where the other stood, so they circled each other warily.

"If I'd known Connecticut was under water most of the time, I wouldn't have even come for this damned audition," Colin grumbled that afternoon. He was slouched in a wing chair in the living room, one leg thrown negligently over the arm of the chair as he stared disconsolately out at the pouring rain.

"If I'd known you were coming to Connecticut," Gina shot back, "I'd have moved to Outer Mongolia."

"I wish I'd written and told you," Colin said soulfully. "Maybe then I'd have gotten the job just for myself, the way I deserve it."

"Keep this up," Gina said sweetly, "and you'll *get* the job just for yourself, the way you deserve it."

"So you're still thinking of finking out on me, eh, Longford?"

Gina sighed loudly. She was trying to knit an afghan for her niece and the yarn persisted in raveling. She swore at it then lifted wry eyes to her companion. "No, Colin, I'm not thinking of finking out on you. That was an idle threat. I signed that contract, and I mean to fulfill my part of it. You can stop worrying that I'll prove as faithless as every other woman you've ever known."

"What makes you think every woman I've known was faithless?" Colin asked. "Women don't walk out on *me*, Gina. I walk out on *them*."

"Except for Sally," Gina said dryly. She almost would have laughed at his openly macho stance, except she suspected there was true pain beneath it, and not for all the money in the world would she have made fun of a person in pain.

An uncomfortable look crossed his face and he cleared his throat. "Sally was different."

She nodded to herself. She was right—he was in pain. "In what way was she different?"

He sighed, rubbing his face tiredly. "Let's not talk about it, okay?"

"No, it's not okay," Gina said. "We're partners now, whether we like it or not. I want to get to know you. Tell me about Sally. That seems to be a good place to start."

"Just because we're partners doesn't mean we have to get to know each other."

"You sure seemed interested in getting to know me earlier today," Gina chided. "Does this mean I can take the bar off my bedroom door tonight?"

"Carnal knowledge is one thing," Colin said. "Personal knowledge is quite another."

"Tell me, oh Sage of the Desert, just where does one draw the line between the two?"

"In bed," Colin answered, one corner of his mouth lifted in a confident grin.

"You almost tempt me," Gina said, smiling for the first time. "You act so damned cocksure of yourself, as if you're the best thing in bed since Rhett Butler, that I almost regret not taking you up on your offer."

"You *will* take me up on it." She stared at him, astounded. His quiet confidence threatened to unhinge her. Her temper, which moments ago had seemed completely under control, now threatened to soar. Carefully she put down her knitting and threw another log on the fire then punched it with the poker, taking out her anger on it.

"I get to you, don't I, Longford," Colin asked lazily.

She glanced at him, eyes glinting coolly. "You tick me off, if that's what you're asking, yes."

"That's not what I meant and you know it. Those sparks in that fireplace are nothing compared to the ones between us. We're dynamite together, or at least we could be. Get down off that high horse of yours and come to bed with me. We'd burn up the sheets."

She put her hands on her hips and shook her head at him. "You have the most colossal ego," she said with wonder. "How do you fit that head of yours through doorways?"

"When there's only one thing you've ever been successful at in your entire life, you tend to stick to it," he joked.

She frowned, slowly lowering herself into the chair opposite him. What did he mean? He looked like the kind of man who'd been successful at everything he'd done. Why was he implying he'd only been successful with women? She decided to play him along, just to see what kind of response she'd get. "Yes," she said artlessly, examining her nails, "it must be difficult for you. I'll bet you're not used to striking out with the ladies." She looked up, her green eyes wide and innocent. "Tell me, what else have you done with your life besides seduce women?"

He looked as if he were going to laugh out loud, as if he found her questions highly amusing, but he only said, "One time I was a pretty good stunt man in Hollywood, but then I went and did a damn fool thing and broke a few important bones and the docs wouldn't let me go back to work, but other than that, I don't think you could say I've been particularly successful at anything."

Gina's face took on a thoughtful look. He was covering up, of course. Laughter like his usually hid a million tears. But why? Didn't his job as movie reviewer for the largest paper in New Mexico count for anything? It was comparable to hers, and she considered herself a success. Why would it be so different for a man?

Then it hit her what else he'd just said. She knitted her brow, searching her memory. Slowly light dawned. "Of course!" she said triumphantly. "You *were* a great stunt man! The best in the business, some said. Colin Cassidy! I should have remembered! That stunt you did when you doubled for Ryan Tracy in *Diablo Nights*, where you drove a burning truck through a police barrier then rolled out of the driver's seat on fire, is a classic. I was on the edge of my seat, shoveling popcorn into my mouth, I was so excited. I remember I spilled my drink and didn't even notice until I found out you were safe.''

Colin looked at her admiringly. "You really *do* know your movie history, don't you? That was almost ten years ago.''

"What's ten years when it comes to a stunt like that? You made movie history more than once with your work. You paved the way for the great stunts that we're seeing now.'' She sat back, her eyes shining. "I'm impressed, Cassidy. I'm really impressed!''

He shook his head self-deprecatingly. "Ancient history, Longford. Those were the glory days. They're gone now, and they ain't comin' back.'' He lapsed into a brooding silence, and Gina stared at him thoughtfully.

"You still didn't tell me what happened with Sally.''

He chuckled ruefully. "Persistent, aren't you?''

"I guess you could say that,'' she admitted. "So tell me— why'd you two break up?''

He waved his hand at her. "C'mon, Longford, forget it, will you?''

"No, Colin, I won't,'' she said, chin raised determinedly. "I keep getting the feeling there's something you're hiding and I want to know what it is. You're my partner now, and I don't want any unpleasant surprises cropping up in the middle of our contract. A man doesn't just get fired from his job and drive halfway across country to an audition for another job without there being some underlying reason. What gives, Colin? I have a right to know.''

Colin sighed long-sufferingly and hoisted his booted leg over the chair arm. He stretched his long legs out in front of him and said, "Okay, I'll tell you, but don't expect me to cave in on everything. A man's got a right to some privacy, you know.''

Gina smiled patiently. "So what's the story?"

Colin's face grew serious as he contemplated the fire that roared in the grate. "I'm in hock up to my ears, Gina," he said at last. "After I broke my back and couldn't do stunt work anymore, I wandered home to New Mexico and found work related to the only thing I know—movies. I reviewed movies for any little rag that printed reviews. I got lucky. I *know* the movie business, Gina, from the inside, where it counts. Luckily, I can write a decent story, so I slowly worked up to lead reviewer at the *Desert Enquirer*.

"About that time, the publisher's daughter came home from a broken marriage back East. Sally Jennings isn't the smartest woman on earth, but she's one of the prettiest and the sexiest, and she understands men. She also can't live without them. She fastened her big brown eyes on me and that was it. I was a sitting duck. Next thing you know, I took all my savings from what I'd earned in Hollywood and bought us a big house in the hills outside Albuquerque and we were living together.

"Things went well for a while," he continued, "then my younger sister, Debbie, got in a bad car accident. She didn't have any health insurance, so she couldn't pay the bills. I took out a humongous mortgage on my house and got some of Debbie's biggest bills paid off, and things were going okay until it hit me one day that Sally was coming home later and later every night, smelling of expensive booze and a man's cologne I wouldn't be caught dead wearing.''

Colin sighed and closed his eyes. Watching him, Gina felt her heart go out to him. He looked exhausted and, even worse, humiliated, and all because she'd dragged this story out of him; she felt like the biggest heel on earth.

"Look, Colin," she said quietly, "you don't have to tell me any more. I get the picture."

He opened his eyes and lifted his head, piercing her with his black gaze. "You wanted the story, Longford, so you're getting it. Now just sit there and listen."

Gina sat back, stunned at the venom in his tone. It was clear he resented her questions and truly felt like a failure. Gina wished now she'd never pried into his background. Her curiosity was only forcing them further apart, not bringing them closer to understanding each other. "All right, Colin," she said quietly, "I'm listening."

Colin looked away from her, staring moodily at the rain that continued to pour from the heavens as he went on with his story. "I found out that Sally was carrying on behind my back, and I asked her to move out, but like a fool, I'd put the house in both our names and her daddy got her a big-shot lawyer who told her to stay put, so *I* moved out. I wasn't about to stay in the same house while she was carrying on right under my nose.

"So there I was, with a huge house on a mountaintop that *she* was living in, with a sister who needed my financial assistance and me without a job." He cocked a wry glance at Gina. "Sally's new boyfriend had moved in with her and she convinced her daddy that it wouldn't be very comfortable for her if I were still working on his paper, so he canned me." He heaved a sigh. "So then I saw the ad for the job as host of this new syndicated movie review show and I felt like getting out of New Mexico, so I packed my bags and set out for Connecticut. I was almost to Pennsylvania when my engine conked out on me, so I bought that wreck I left in New Haven and continued the journey, and that's the sorry story of Colin Cassidy, has-been and ne'er-do-well." He cocked a glance at her. "Satisfied?"

She met his gaze placidly. "Has-been and ne'er-do-well?" she asked quietly. "You were one of the best stunt men in Hollywood, and because of a freak accident, you couldn't continue working. Then you go home and work your way up to movie reviewer on the top paper in Albuquerque. Now, you've just talked your way into becoming cohost of an up-and-coming new television program, and you call yourself a has-been and ne'er-do-well?"

She stood up and walked toward the French doors, folding her arms stiffly and staring out at the pouring rain. "Sounds to me like you have a big case of self-pity, Cassidy. You've been successful at everything you do, yet you're letting that Sally woman destroy your self-esteem." She turned to face him, eyes flashing angrily. "The world's a tough place, Cassidy. Start giving yourself a little credit for what you've done instead of constantly looking at the dark side."

With that, she turned and stalked from the room, but at the kitchen door, he caught up with her. He gripped her arm and turned her to face him.

"Slow down, woman," he said. "Maybe a guy would like to talk to you a little more."

Gina's throat suddenly went dry. "Well, maybe a woman wouldn't like to talk to you," she said, her voice shaking. He was too close, too potently masculine, and she couldn't seem to get enough air. She had to get away. Pushing hard against his chest, she tried to break his grip, but he merely chuckled and drew her closer.

"Ornery little filly, aren't you?" he asked, affection ringing in his low voice. He smoothed a path through her rumpled hair with his large hand then settled it around the nape of her neck. He mesmerizingly rubbed the skin beneath her ear with his thumb until she was shaking so hard she felt she might slide right out of his hands.

"What are you doing?" she asked, forced to cling to him lest her knees buckle.

"Getting to know you a little better," he drawled easily.

"Let go of me, Cassidy," she said unsteadily. "I told you once, I don't like macho men. You're big and strong and good-looking and you think every woman on the face of the earth is ready to fall into bed with you at the first opportunity, but you're wrong."

"I know that," he said easily.

"You do?" she asked, surprised.

"Sure," he said, grinning. "I know every woman on the face of the earth doesn't want to go to bed with me. It's you I'm sure about. You *do* want to go to bed with me, but you're too stubborn to admit it. Stubborn or scared, I can't figure out which."

"Why should I be scared?" she demanded, wondering if he felt her trembling.

"I don't know," he mused, his head to one side as he studied her through slitted eyes. "But we'll talk about that later. Right now, I've got much more important things on my mind."

"Such as?"

"Such as this," he said, pulling her closer. He lowered his head and suddenly his lips were on hers, enticing and probing, not gentle but not fierce, either. His kiss took her breath away, and when she made the fatal mistake of opening her mouth to tell him to stop, his tongue stole into her mouth and she was lost.

Everything that had been pent up threatened to burst inside her. She felt like a flower ready to blossom. Shaking, she clung to him, letting him kiss her, letting his tongue circle hers, letting his strong arms press her into his hard body. She balled her hands into fists at the collar of his shirt and clung to him, refusing to kiss him back but not fighting him off, either. She felt a mighty wall of desire rising up inside her like a tidal wave. It came crashing toward her, rising up and up, threatening her entire life, yet she couldn't fight it, couldn't turn and run. She was locked in Colin Cassidy's arms, and whatever he demanded, she seemed helpless to refuse.

He ran his large hand caressingly up and down her side, and she could only draw in a quick, unsteady breath, then give herself up to the pleasure that cascaded over her. His touch felt so good, so right. It was like rain on a parched desert, like food after nine days of starvation. Her body shook and she could only cling to him, eyes closed, head back as he ran his tongue down the slim length of her neck and into the hollow of her throat.

"Sweet," he whispered raggedly into her throat. "You taste as sweet as honey."

"Oh God," she moaned. "We've got to stop."

"Why?" he whispered, dropping gentle kisses along her neck. "Why do we have to stop? Any law that says we can't kiss each other?"

"I ... We ..." She struggled to find an answer, but none came. His breath was warm and sweet on her neck as he dotted a lazy path of kisses toward her ear. Then he began to nibble on her earlobe and she felt a shaft of pleasure sweep through her.

"No," she whispered hoarsely as he guided her carefully toward the couch in front of the fireplace.

"Yes," he crooned in her ear. "Yes."

She was on the couch before she knew it and he was beside her. She couldn't stop him now if she had to. He rubbed his hands up and down her back, pressing her into his hard body, sending erotic pleasure messages to her brain, which in turn transmitted pulsing signals to the rest of her body. She grew warm and restive, found herself pushing closer to his warmth, wanting suddenly to unbutton his shirt and run her hand over his hairy chest, wanting to feel the smooth skin beneath the curls, to run her palms along the hard muscles in pleasurable examination.

She swallowed painfully and told herself to fight the attraction that sizzled between them, but her body was too willful, and she was too needy. She was a woman, not a rock. She needed this glorious pleasure, this wondrous sensuality. Her body cried out for it, trembled with desire, and she was helpless to fight it.

"Oh, yes," she moaned, eyes closed, head back.

"You like it," he said.

"Yes," she whispered brokenly.

"You want more?" he murmured.

She nodded, her eyes still closed. She couldn't look at him, couldn't let him see the rapture in her eyes. She was still too ashamed at the wanton way she was succumbing to his advances, still too shocked by her own response.

"Tell me what you want, Gina," he murmured softly. "Tell me every place you want me to touch, to kiss, tell me every little thing you want me to do."

"I..." She felt choked, frightened by the low intensity of his voice, but frightened more by her own need. "I can't."

"Tell me," he persisted, his lips brushing softly, coaxingly against her lips.

"I want you to hold me," she whispered haltingly, opening her eyes to look at him. "I just want to be held."

He stared down at her, his eyes as dark as obsidian, then he slowly released her, looking slightly confused. "You admit it, then. You want a physical relationship as much as I do."

She sat quietly, then nodded. "Yes," she finally murmured.

He rubbed his jaw and stared at the fireplace, his brow furrowed into worry lines.

She watched him, and a slow smile curved her lips. "It's not as easy as you thought it'd be, is it, Cassidy? You can't just drag me by the hair to the nearest bed and have your way with me, can you? What happened? Did it suddenly hit you we'll be working together and it might get a bit awkward between us on the set once the passion's worn off?"

"Not quite," he said, turning to look at her, his eyes still filled with puzzlement. "But I did realize one thing—what we want isn't the same thing. I want to make love to you, and you just want to be held. There's a world of difference there, Gina. I want a woman. You just want a father."

She gasped and turned her head toward the fireplace. The flames licked the logs, leaping and crackling, sending their smoky aroma into the room. She drew her legs up under her and sat huddled in the corner of the couch, trembling not from the cold but from the emotions that warred within her. She ached for his touch, but she hugged herself tightly, trying to restrain the anger that gnawed at her insides.

All men were alike, she decided. They didn't understand a woman's basic need for physical touching. They didn't understand that a woman couldn't just fall into the nearest bed and be done with it. A woman wanted both physical and emotional closeness, and often that began with simply being held by a man. Why couldn't they understand this need? Jack, her ex-husband, never could, and now Colin Cassidy couldn't, either. They always misinterpreted a woman's needs. It was as if men and women spoke two separate emotional languages.

She felt all her hopes slide into an abyss of darkness. There wasn't any chance for men and women, no chance at all. They were destined to misunderstand each other, to fight the battle of the sexes until the end of the world. She struggled to hold back tears of desolation, then rallied, knowing she had to salvage this wreckage in some way.

"I'm so ashamed," she said at last, her cheeks burning. "There hasn't been anyone in a long time. This . . . We . . ." She closed her eyes and rested her forehead on her up-drawn knees. "Oh God, what a mess."

He moved to the other end of the couch, stretching out his long legs and crossing them at the ankles. "Oh, I don't think it's as bad as all that," he said easily.

She shuddered. She was mortified at how she'd acted. How could she face him? "You're a man," she accused coldly. "Men take their release where they can get it. It's not as easy for a woman."

"No? I thought you modern women went to bed with anyone at the drop of a hat."

Her head came up, her eyes sparkling dangerously. "I don't sleep around," she said coolly. "I never have and never will. I don't think there's anything wrong with sex, but I still believe there has to be caring between the man and woman. Otherwise, we're no better than animals."

"That's where you've made your mistake," he said, rising slowly and looking down at her from what seemed an amazing height.

Her eyes snapped with angry fire. "You think it would be all right for us to just . . . just . . . *couple*, here on the floor, like jungle animals?"

"No, Gina, that's not what I meant at all. I mean you've assumed we don't care for each other. *That's* where you made your mistake."

With that amazing statement, he walked abruptly from the room, leaving her staring after him, openmouthed and completely confused.

Eight

Colin was baiting his line with a hook, Gina decided, and she would have to use all her wits to avoid it. In an effort to work off her physical frustration, she tied an old scarf around her head and waded into the kitchen pantry and began cleaning. Boxes of food were flung from their shelves, bags of flour flew out the pantry door, brooms and mops and cleaning items clattered, and the dust flew. The noise was ear-shattering, and the entire time she muttered and cursed under her breath, wishing she could be cool and refined and wave away Colin's passes at her with a charming laugh, like the sophisticated woman she'd always wanted to be.

Gina sighed and rubbed a hand across her nose, leaving a wide streak of dirt behind. The only trouble was, she wasn't sophisticated, wasn't in the least knowledgeable about how to contain her emotions. It was her biggest failing, this inheritance from her Italian mother. Why couldn't she have inherited her father's cool English manner, his flinty eyes and glacial calm? Instead, she'd taken everything from her mother—her dark, exotic coloring, her penchant for gypsy-style clothing, her emotional outbursts and tirades. For years, Gina had struggled to subdue her emotions just as she'd struggled to subdue her hair, but it was useless.

She did a pretty good job of hiding her real self most of the time. At work she was cool and professional and she felt in control of her life, but for some reason, Colin Cassidy had snuck behind her facade and found her out, and she was miserable. She felt just as she had when she was married— vulnerable, emotional, out of control. She *hated* it.

Cursing, she threw a box of rice across the kitchen, where it bounced off the refrigerator and landed on the floor with a solid thud, scattering rice in all directions.

"Temper, temper," Colin said, chuckling softly from the doorway.

Her head shot up and she stared at him defiantly. "Oh, go soak your head," she grumbled.

"And undo all the terrific nursing you've done? I feel like a new man. My cold is gone and I feel as if I could take on the world."

"Be my guest," she said curtly, turning back to her cleaning. "At least that would get you out of my hair."

"Speaking of your hair, what have you done to it?"

She remembered the old scarf she'd tied over her thick, unruly hair and glared at Colin. "I'm cleaning, Colin. It's something you no doubt have no experience with, but we who believe in hygiene quite often indulge ourselves. It wards off bubonic plague and typhus and other assorted killer diseases. When I clean, I tie my hair back. Now if you don't mind, I'm busy." She slipped past him and began to fill a pail with hot water and cleaning fluid.

"I can think of better ways to spend a rainy afternoon."

A thrill went through her, which she repressed. "Can you?" she asked sarcastically. "So can I, but I'll bet it's a far bet from what you have in mind. I'd planned to attend a matinee this afternoon. The new Alentejo film is out."

"I hate Alentejo."

"You would."

"What's that supposed to mean?"

"You have no taste. Alentejo is the Spanish Bergman. He's an artist. He has a vision. He has soul." She glanced disdainfully at Colin, who lounged against the wall sipping a beer. "Unlike a certain reviewer I know."

"Come to bed with me and I'll show you soul."

She rolled her eyes and dropped the sponge into the bucket. "*Everything* gets back to sex with you, doesn't it, Cassidy?" she asked. "I mean, everything! Sally probably left you because she couldn't stand being mauled ten times a day."

"You're really hung up on Sally, aren't you?" he asked. "Tell me, Longford, what was your husband like?"

"None of your business," she said tersely, attacking the pantry shelves with the sponge.

"That's hardly fair, Gina," Colin said. "After all, you made me tell you about Sally. We're partners, remember?"

She scrubbed defiantly, refusing to answer until Colin stepped into the small pantry. Suddenly the room seemed to shrink. She swallowed thickly and stopped scrubbing, staring down at the wet sponge in her hand, unable to continue working.

"Something the matter, Longford?" Colin asked softly.

She swallowed again and began to talk as fast as she could. "My husband was a typical male—brought up by a doting mother to expect that supper would be on the table promptly at five, that his socks would be washed, dried and folded, and placed perfectly in the lower-right-hand corner of his fifth dresser drawer. By *me*. He hadn't the least understanding of my needs as a woman or a human being. He liked the idea that I worked and brought in a second paycheck but wouldn't think of helping me clean house or cook. Between both 'jobs' I worked and slaved fifteen hours a day, and he worked eight then came home—*when* he deigned to—and lay on the couch reading the paper or watching television while I waited on him.''

She rinsed the sponge in the cleaning liquid and went back to scrubbing vigorously, taking her anger out on the dirty shelves. "He believed in the divine right of kings, in male supremacy and in female bondage. I was his slave, according to him, and he was my master—I was his to control. When he wanted sex, he snapped his fingers and expected me to roll over and accommodate him.''

She glanced at Colin to see how her tirade was affecting him. His face showed nothing, neither amusement nor anger. He looked neutral, but interested.

"I vowed when I left him,'' Gina continued, "that I'd never get involved with another macho man as long as I lived, and look what happened. I go around a corner and bump into the macho-est man I've ever met and we end up working and living together.''

"Just deserts,'' he said, smiling.

She tossed her head and rinsed the sponge again. "The vengeance of a wrathful god is more like it.''

"Why'd you marry him in the first place? You must have loved him once.''

Gina stared down at the sponge in her hand, remembering. "Yes,'' she finally admitted. "Once I did, before...''

"Before what?''

She shrugged. "Before I realized how impossible it is for men and women to live together, for love to survive.''

"So you took yourself out of the running," Colin said. "You threw up your hands and gave up, just like that. Like a spoiled little kid, when the game didn't go your way, you took your dolls and went home and refused to play anymore."

Gina rounded on him, green eyes blazing. "That's not true!" she shouted. "You're twisting things around. It wasn't a game. It was a *marriage*, and he...he..." She turned her back on Colin, aghast that tears were threatening to overflow and run down her cheeks.

"He what, Gina?" Colin asked, sounding almost gentle.

She wiped the back of her hand across her cheeks and waved away his question. "Oh, it doesn't matter," she said, her voice shaking precariously. "It was a long time ago and it's over now. I just want to forget it."

"You may want to, but it sounds like it's as raw as the day your marriage ended. Maybe what you need is to talk about it, get it out of your system once and for all."

"I don't want to talk about it," she said, attacking the next pantry shelf.

"But you need to."

"I don't!"

"You do!"

She rounded on him, eyes glittering with unshed tears. "He cheated on me!" she yelled. "There! Are you satisfied?"

He stared at her, his face confused, then he lowered his eyes and said, "Excuse me. I won't bother you anymore." Then he turned and left.

Gina stared after him then let her shoulders slump and sat down on an upturned box, staring balefully out the pantry door. A fine mess she'd made. She didn't seem to have the knack for communicating with men, only for shouting at them and fighting with them. This scene with Colin was a replay of a hundred fights with Jack. She closed her eyes and rubbed her forehead, wondering if the failure of her marriage wasn't just as much her fault as Jack's. This was the first time she'd ever allowed herself to face that possibility, and it shook her to the core. She opened her eyes and stared wearily at the kitchen, littered now with the contents of the pantry.

She remembered cleaning this way when she was married to Jack and cursing him roundly for not helping. But she'd never asked him to help, not even once. She'd expected him to help automatically. Maybe, she suddenly realized, that was like expecting a tiger to stop eating meat and prefer vanilla pudding.

What if she'd gone to Jack and taken his hand and cuddled up next to him and explained how she felt? What if she'd stopped yelling long enough to listen to him? Once again, she cursed her temper. If only she could learn to rein it in, to hold back the hot words and accusations, to *talk* instead of yell. Maybe then their marriage would have survived.

But no. She couldn't forgive Jack for his flings with other women. One affair she might have forgiven, but there were dozens. She was always coming across the evidence of his infidelities—lipstick smudges on his shirts and handkerchiefs, bills for intimate meals at romantic restaurants and out-of-the-way hotel rooms, for dozens of roses, bottles of wine and champagne, for sexy underwear, none of which she ever saw. With each infidelity, it was as if he opened a wound and rubbed it with salt.

But Jack Longford was a handsome man, a virile man. He attracted women the way honey attracted ants. He'd always tried to make peace with her by saying he loved lots of women but she was the only one he'd ever married. But that hadn't been enough. She wanted more than his ring on her finger and his last name. She'd wanted his love, his loyalty, his fidelity. She'd wanted to trust him.

Now, sitting in the pantry, she wondered if she'd lost forever the ability to trust a man. Was there nothing for her but this antiseptic life she'd created? Couldn't she have it all?

She stood up slowly, painfully, and dipped the sponge into the bucket of cleaning fluid. By now, the liquid had grown cold and she'd lost her desire to scrub and clean. She wanted to take a hot bath and then search out Colin Cassidy. She wanted, just once more before she grew old and gray, to have a night of passion with a virile man.

Biting her lip, Gina stood and contemplated her thoughts, then slowly she set about cleaning the pantry. She was entitled to it, dammit. It had been a long time since she'd gone to bed with a man, too long. Maybe she could find a way to do it gracefully.

She shook her head. No, it was impossible. Then she lifted her head and stared unseeingly into space, remembering the dark hair on his chest, the way one corner of his mouth curved in a grin, the way he'd slid his hand between her legs that morning in bed....

Startled, she shook herself and set about cleaning again, scrubbing the shelves with all the energy she could muster. She would need to work herself to the bone, completely exhaust herself. That way, she would fall into bed tonight and sleep like a baby. That way, no visions of Colin would haunt her. That way, she would be safe.

Safe, Gina reflected bitterly later, but certainly not very happy. She stood examining the immaculate pantry, where all the spices were lined up alphabetically, the cans and boxes set in rows graduated by height, the pots and pans nested artfully, neatly, looking like the stockroom in the world's best organized corporation. For some reason, she didn't find her finished work fulfilling. She was still thinking about Colin, about the way he'd kissed her, so gentle yet so insistent. She shivered a little and wished she hadn't ever stopped on the way to the audition. Why couldn't she have satisfied herself with an irate toot of her horn and left him behind in a cloud of fallen autumn leaves? Why did she always give in to the temper that simmered just beneath what she had always wished was a decorous surface?

Tiredly she unwrapped the scarf from her head and trudged toward her bedroom. She needed that bath. Now. She needed to sink into the hot, scented water and let it rinse away all the hurt and disappointment, for right now her heart ached far worse than her body.

The problem was, she wasn't facing the problem. Not really. She was dodging it, rationalizing her reactions to Colin, trying to force herself to behave one way when her ornery body persisted in reacting another.

Irritably Gina slammed the door to her bedroom. As she wandered around the room, she began undressing. She dropped her blouse on the floor and realized what the problem was: she was physically attracted to Colin Cassidy. No, she was more than physically attracted to him, she was devoured by attraction to him, inundated by it, lost in an unruly sea of gnashing teeth and howling hormones.

She shed her jeans and stood gnawing on her thumbnail. Okay, so where did that leave her? Alone in her own home with the most attractive man she'd met in years. The only problem was, she couldn't stand him. He represented all she detested in men. He was egotistical, dominating, rude, arrogant, and he hated women.

Throwing up her hands, she sat on her bed and rested her heels on the bed frame, then put her elbows on her knees and glumly set her chin in her hands. Talk about quandaries! She could go to bed with him and forever hate herself afterward, or she could resist her physical needs and compensate by feeling virtuous.

Some compensation, she thought rebelliously, regarding her bed with belligerent eyes. Right now, the last thing she felt like being was holier-than-anyone. Right now, she just wanted sex! She was a modern woman, guaranteed the right to physical pleasure by birth control devices and her ability to take care of herself. Why shouldn't she just go ahead and take her pleasure when it presented itself?

Then she moved uneasily. Something remotely puritanical stirred in her conscience, and she realized that she wasn't quite as modern as she made herself out to be. When she'd told Colin earlier today that she wanted to care for the man she made love with, she'd meant it. Sex without love or at least affection was ultimately empty.

So. That left her with jogging in place, working out on her rowing machine and riding her stationary bicycle. By then, she would be so tired she wouldn't care if Cary Grant, Paul Newman and Robert Redford were all waiting for her in the next room, much less Colin Cassidy.

After exercising for an hour and a half, Gina took a hot bath and washed her hair, then let it air dry as she painted her toe- and fingernails. Then she padded around her room naked, straightening here, dusting there, trying to figure out why she wasn't as tired as she'd hoped she would be. She caught sight of herself in the mirror and came to a halt.

Her hair curled around her head like a dark halo, and her skin was as golden as that of a South Seas maiden. She had round, firm breasts, a tiny waist and flaring hips that tapered into smooth, silken thighs and calves.

She felt a wave of sensuality move through her and she turned away from the mirror, sick with frustrated desire. Hurriedly she put on a beige lace teddy, her fingers shaking as she fastened the tiny row of buttons that marched down its front. Then she found her black velour robe and belted it tightly around her slim middle. With Colin safely in the guest room, she could sneak into the kitchen and warm some milk, then build a fire. Perhaps then, lulled by the heat of the fire, warmed by the ancient child's remedy for insomnia, she could find surcease from this ache that permeated her body and kept her pacing her room.

She shut her bedroom door softly, glancing hastily at Colin's door. Under it, a thin strip of light glowed. Reassured that he was indeed in his room, she tiptoed silently down the dark hall, wishing she'd thought to wear slippers. Sighing silently, she resigned herself to cold feet until she stepped down into the living room, where the soft Oriental carpet underfoot immediately warmed her.

Without turning on any lights, she crossed the expansive room, shivering a little at the unaccustomed darkness, and entered the kitchen, making sure the door was closed before she turned on the lights. Quickly and efficiently she set about heating milk, then found a bag of chocolate chip cookies and emptied the contents onto a plate. After pouring the steaming milk into a mug, she set both on a tray and headed toward the living room, careful to turn off the light switch with her elbow as she left the kitchen and let the door swing shut behind her.

In the living room, she hesitated for just a moment, feeling strangely eerie. She wasn't used to wandering around her home in the dark. She lived far off the main road and kept her home well-lit at night, having found that bright lights did more to make her feel safe than the alarm system that was hooked into the local police station.

But now she shivered, feeling a presence in the room that shook her to the core. She looked around, but her eyes weren't yet accustomed enough to the dark for her to see clearly. Only an occasional bulky shape of a piece of furniture rose in the gloom before her.

Reassured, Gina walked toward the fireplace. Kneeling, she rested the tray on the raised hearth then set about lighting the birch logs that rested on the grate. When the fire was crackling, she sat back on the rug and looked around. Rather than helping her see better, the light from the fireplace seemed to make the rest of the room even darker. She was illuminated clearly in the small circle of light radiating from the fireplace, but the rest of the room seemed pitched into complete blackness.

Again she shivered, telling herself she was being fanciful, yet she couldn't escape the conviction that someone was there, watching her. Perhaps someone was outside the French doors, standing in the shadows of the dripping bushes, staring in at her even while the rain continued to pour from the black skies.

She felt her throat tighten with tension and rubbed her arms, but her black velour robe and the now-roaring fire did little to chase away the chill she felt. Hurriedly she picked up the mug of warm milk and raised it to her mouth with trembling fingers. She was about to take a sip when something stirred in the darkness behind her.

Fear flooded her as goose bumps broke out on her skin and a ripple of tension ran up her spine. She looked around, but nothing was there—at least nothing she could detect. But her eyes were becoming more accustomed to the dark, and she could make out the friendly forms of her couch and the wing chair next to the fireplace and the one near the windows—

She went very still. Her heart started hammering, knocking painfully against her breast even as her breath caught in her lungs then was expelled on a gasp of fear. There was someone in here, someone sitting in the wing chair by the

French doors. She could just make out his form, even though he was slumped in the chair so that his head wasn't outlined above the top. She knew it was a male figure, knew even though she couldn't make out who it was. There was something terribly threatening about that large male shape that blended with the chair, just discernible, yet oddly undetectable....

"You scared the living daylights out of me when you first walked through here, you know," a male voice said from the depths of the chair.

Gina screamed and dropped the mug of milk. It landed on the stone hearth, shattering the quiet of the room and splattering the milk all over the floor and herself.

"Are you all right?" the voice asked, then the form rose from the chair and Colin Cassidy materialized before her eyes.

"You!" she cried, staring at him with wide, frightened eyes.

"Yes," Colin said, sauntering toward her, his hands thrust easily into his jeans pockets. "Me."

He came to a stop in front of her, and all she could do was sit on the floor and stare up at him, her gaze traveling up and up and up, past the snug jeans that covered his well-muscled legs, past the silver belt buckle, up to the wide expanse of bare flesh that was his chest.

Her gaze rested on his muscular chest a moment, taking in the dark swirls of hair, then rose again, up past his neck to the strong chin, the sensuous lips, the slightly crooked nose, until it came to rest on his eyes.

They were darker than midnight, yet strange lights seemed to shine in them. She told herself it was only the reflection of the fire from the fireplace, but she shivered nonetheless.

"I'm sorry if I frightened you," Colin said, "but it's only fair. You scared the bejesus out of me when you appeared like a dark apparition in the doorway and drifted across the room without making a sound. Dressed all in black like that, you looked like an evil spirit. I actually broke out in goose bumps.''

"Did you.'' Her voice, she was proud to note, was low and controlled. She might have been making polite conversation at high tea in a posh Boston hotel. Bending, she began to gather up the shards of broken mug, but Colin quickly knelt and took her hand.

"Careful,'' he cautioned. "You might cut yourself.''

She stared down at his hand on hers, then slowly raised her eyes to his. "Let go of me,'' she said, but this time there was a quivering note in her voice. She hoped he didn't catch it. She wouldn't want him to think she was afraid of him.

The firelight danced in his dark eyes and illuminated the hint of a smile. "I'm only trying to help,'' he said.

"I don't need your help.''

"Oh, but you do,'' he countered. "Your lovely black robe is completely spattered with—what is that—milk? And you're shivering. I can feel you trembling. The fire isn't warm enough yet to heat you. Perhaps you'd better take that off before you catch a chill.''

"My robe is fine.''

"I think not.''

His voice was so low-pitched she could barely hear his words. There was something in it that made her shiver again, something disturbingly sensual, as if he were setting out to seduce her and planned to do it solely by speech.

"You see?'' he said, amusement threading his deep voice. "You *are* shivering. Take off that robe and I'll get you another.''

"I don't have another.''

He stared into her eyes. "No?''

She stared back, her heart hammering, the pulse in the hollow of her throat throbbing painfully.

"Then perhaps I can do for you what you did for me," he said. "Return the favor, as it were."

"The favor?" She stared at him, confused by his words. What was he saying?

He reached out and slid his hand around the back of her neck and began to slowly massage it. "You're tense," he observed. "The muscles in your neck are knotted."

"What favor?" she persisted. Somewhere in the depths of her subconscious, she knew what he was talking about, but her mind refused to face it. She had to ask him again. "What favor?"

"Why, don't you remember? You kept me warm when I was shivering. It's only fair that I do the same for you now." He reached out and began to untie the cords of her robe. She clutched at his hands.

"No," she whispered.

He loosened the cord then ran his hands up the lapels of her robe. "Yes," he murmured softly, pushing the robe off her bare shoulders. "I think yes...."

Nine

Colin slid one finger beneath the slim strap of Gina's beige satin teddy and gently tugged it off her shoulder. Gina shivered from the touch of his finger against her skin.

"You see?" he said again, dropping a soft kiss on her shoulder, "you really are shivering."

"I don't want you to do this," she said in a tortured whisper, but she dipped her head to the side to allow his lips the freedom to peruse her neck and shoulder.

"Yes, you do," he whispered huskily, his breath warm and moist near her ear. "Just for once, Gina, be honest with me. This is what you want and it's what I want. There isn't any use in pretending any longer. I can see how hard your nipples are. This satin leaves very little to my fertile imagination. I can hear how hard you're breathing. I know you liked it when I kissed your shoulder. You didn't push me away."

He ran his hand beneath the rich thickness of her dark hair and sighed softly. "My God, I love your hair. When your hat fell off by my car and your hair tumbled out from beneath it, my heart stopped. I wanted to reach out and pull you into my arms and run my fingers through it. I knew what you were like from the moment I saw your hair. It's you, Gina—unruly, abandoned, crackling with intensity and snapping with electricity, but confined too long under a restricting cover." His dark eyes roamed her face admiringly, a small smile playing at the corners of his lips. "The cover is off now, Gina. Let yourself go. Take what you want from life. Don't run from it."

She stared into his dark eyes and felt a rising warmth inside her, felt the sweet, aching call of desire, the call she'd pretended not to hear, the one that told her she was a woman, with a woman's longings, a woman's needs.

Slowly she reached out and ran her fingertips down his brawny chest, savoring the warmth of his skin, the pleasant sensation of its roughness against her fingertips. His clean scent invaded her senses, making her head reel with pleasure.

"That's right," he coaxed, "touch me. Kiss me, Gina. Hold me."

At those words, she lifted her head. "Hold you?" she murmured, her eyes filled with painful questions. "Earlier today I told you I wanted to be held, and you told me I wanted a father, not a man. But now it's okay for you to want to be held?"

His eyes filled with shadows and he looked away, his face troubled. He ran his hand roughly through his dark hair and stared into the fireplace. "You changed everything when you said that, Gina," he finally said.

"Changed everything?" she asked, truly puzzled.

He looked back at her, meeting her eyes. "I wanted it to be simple, uncomplicated. No feelings, no involvement. But when you said that, when you raised your eyes and looked up at me, you looked so *trusting*, so...so vulnerable—" He broke off and let out a frustrated sigh. "Look, I'm not much good at explaining my feelings. All I know is, you suddenly weren't just a beautiful body, you were a person, a human being with needs of her own. You jolted me, Gina, and I hit back in the only way I knew how."

"But *why*?" she asked, in confusion. She couldn't understand this man, couldn't fathom why it was suddenly so terribly important that she did.

"Why?" He chuckled ruefully. "I told you, because I didn't want to get involved. I wanted it to be quick and easy, with no strings attached. But when you told me you wanted me to hold you, you made it everything I hadn't wanted. You made it human. I wanted out as quick as possible, and insulting you was the best way I knew to get out."

She turned away and stared into the flickering flames, disappointment radiating through her like the pain of a toothache. "And now you're back," she said bitterly, "all sweet talk and trying one more time for a quick fling."

"No," he said, "not this time."

His words shook her. She looked back at him and met his dark gaze. He didn't shrink from her eyes, didn't look away. "What are you saying, Cassidy?" she asked, unable to trust him. Was this just another line, another carefully baited hook?

"I've been thinking about nothing else all afternoon," Colin responded. "I've been pacing my room, thinking about all the ramifications. We're going to be working together, dammit, and the wisest course is exactly what you've been saying—no involvement. But we *are* involved, if only as working partners for the next few months."

He let out a long, frustrated sigh, then went on. "So I asked myself, What are you going to do, Colin? Are you going to pretend she doesn't set your blood on fire every time you see her, or are you going to risk it?"

"Risk it?"

He looked up and met her eyes. "Involvement."

"Is it such a risk?" she asked softly.

He nodded grimly. "For me it is. Gina, I'm—" He broke off and groaned softly. "Oh, Gina, I haven't got a sterling record with women. I've chosen the wrong ones, I see that now. I've always been attracted to the ones who want their names in lights, the prettiest, the most ambitious. But for some reason, at the same time I'm attracted, I start to pull back. Something inside me wants a woman who'll just stay home and cook and clean house and be there for me. Just for *me*, Gina." He shook his head. "I know you can't understand that. To you, that's chauvinism, provincialism. You must feel like turning me in to the National Organization of Women."

Sensing his confusion and pain, Gina reached out to him. Her natural compassion surfaced and she took his hand. "It sounds to me as if you're in the same mess as the rest of us in the world—we want two different things at the same time and can't resolve the conflict. For some reason, you're attracted to ambitious women, yet you hate that about yourself, and you end up hating the woman, too." She cocked her head sideways. "Why, Colin? Why can't you just let the woman be what she is?"

"Because when a woman *is*, when she just goes off and does her thing, she forgets about the man in her life and suddenly everything is her career. Women go overboard, work fifteen hours a day, live for their next promotion, for their power lunches or breakfasts, or whatever's the 'in' thing now."

"And men don't?" Gina asked softly.

He glanced up at her and chuckled ruefully. "Okay, you got me there."

She smiled sadly, resting her chin on her knees and gazing soulfully into the fireplace. "I want two things, too, Colin," she finally said, her voice soft and dreamy. "I want my career, but I also want a man in my life. I'm human, too, not some automaton who lives on computer printouts and daily planner calendars. Sometimes, Colin, I get so lonely. I feel so lost. When I told you I wanted to be held this afternoon, that's exactly what I wanted. The sex could come later—I *wanted* it to come later, but the *holding*—" She broke off, feeling tears well up in her eyes. "Oh, Colin," she whispered brokenly, "being held, the feel of a man's strong arms around me, caring for me, for *me*, Colin. Not just anyone, not just any warm body, but *me*, Eugenia Stella Longford."

Surreptitiously she wiped the back of her hand across her eyes, then went on. She couldn't stop now if she wanted. She'd opened up the gates and the floodwaters of emotion were rolling out, gushing forth, spewing out all the pain and frustration and hidden desire.

"It's like we all *need* someone, you know?" she said softly. "Sometimes I think that if human beings don't touch one another, if we don't reach out and connect in some warm, loving, giving way, we'll all die. We'll disintegrate or evaporate, or just plain disappear off the planet."

"Shrivel up," Colin said.

"Yes." She smiled softly. "Yes, exactly."

Colin reached out and put his arm around her, pulling her closer. "So can I hold you now?" he asked softly. "Just hold you, and be held?"

She nodded, turning into his arms, her eyes misted now with tears of joy. In some basic, deep, elemental way, they'd just connected, and she felt real again, human, reborn from the ashes of her old self. She put her arms around him and hugged him tightly, squeezing her eyes shut and laughing softly as he hugged her back.

"Oh, it feels so *good*," she whispered.

"God, yes," he sighed, running his hands up and down her back, then squeezing her again, hugging her, holding her and rocking her back and forth in his loving embrace. Then he sat back, staring at her in amazement. "Do you know, I think you're the first woman in years I've really just *held*?"

"You mean without putting the make on her?" Gina asked wryly.

"Yeah," he said, grinning. "You've really got my number, don't you, Longford? You got me all figured out and pegged right down to my first and last male urges."

She laughed softly, her eyes sparkling. "Well, you're transparent. I mean, take the first time we met. You were cursing a blue streak, muttering to yourself, and cranky as an old goat who'd missed his supper, and you were the *rudest* man I'd ever met! I could tell right away you were as macho as they come."

"*I* was rude!" he said, stunned. "What about you? My God, woman, you stood over me like some avenging demon, green flames shooting out of your eyes, that pretty little foot of yours tapping out a mean rhythm, hands on your hips as if you'd like nothing more than to haul off and belt me into the next state."

"Okay, okay," she said, laughing harder now. "So we were both rude. But we both had an excuse. You had a flat tire and an important audition, and I had the same audition and I'd come around that curve and almost hit you."

"So you want to put it all down to preaudition nerves and forget it? Start over or something?"

"Start over?" she asked, bemused. "Now how would we do that? We've built up this perfect aversion to each other. Why ruin it now?"

"So you like the fighting, eh?" he asked, grinning as he leaned back on one elbow and stretched his body out full length on the floor, the broken mug and spilled milk forgotten.

She considered his question then nodded thoughtfully. "In a way, I do. You see, Colin, I've always been this hothead who's tried to pretend I'm calm and always in control. Of course, I never am, which only adds fuel to the fire. I feel as if I'm living a double life or something—there's the public Gina Longford, who's cool and calm and sophisticated, and the *real* Gina Longford, who's as hot as they come, all emotions, just simmering beneath the exterior and waiting to explode."

"And for some reason, I let you explode."

She nodded again thoughtfully. "Ye-es, I suppose so, though I have no idea why I feel comfortable exploding with you."

"Simple. Maybe you're just plain comfortable with me."

"Uh-oh," she said, rolling her eyes expressively. "Here comes the line. Next you'll be reaching out and fiddling with my hair, or taking my hand and fondling me."

"Honey, if I fondle you, it's not your hand I'm going to mess with."

She sat back, eyes wide, then burst into enchanted laughter. "Oh, Colin, I think I almost *like* you!"

He stared at her, looking absurdly pleased, then he seemed to shake himself and laughed off her comment. "Oh? And why is that? Does it give you pleasure to go slumming every once in a while?"

"Slumming!" Angry sparks erupted in her eyes. "No, I like you because you're *real*, dammit! You say what's on your mind and don't beat around the bush. It has nothing to do with slumming, as you put it. Come on, Colin," she added, irritation ringing in her voice, "why the hell are you always putting yourself down?"

He paused a moment before answering then said almost reluctantly, "It's a defense mechanism, I guess—always say it yourself before someone else has a chance to."

Gina's anger evaporated. It always did when Colin let himself be vulnerable and human. "You've really been hurt, haven't you?" she said softly, her eyes mirroring her compassion. "I'm sorry, Colin. That Sally sounds like a first-class jerk."

"Oh, it wasn't just Sally," Colin said airily. He glanced at Gina. "I guess I have bad luck with women whose names begin with S." He pillowed his head on his arms and stared thoughtfully up at the ceiling, where firelight danced in eerie patterns. "My mother's first name began with an S."

"Your mother?"

Colin took a deep breath and said, "Savanna Black."

The room grew very quiet, quiet enough that Gina's indrawn breath was clearly audible. "Savanna..." She stared at Colin, stunned. "She's your *mother*?" she finally asked, too riddled with confusion to know what to say. "My God, how many Oscars did she win? Three?"

Colin nodded grimly. "Three for Best Actress. Two for Supporting Actress. Twelve nominations in all. She was a hell of an actress. She ran off when I was about six and made straight for Hollywood. She accomplished a lot in twenty years, didn't she?"

"But—" Gina stared, confused more than ever. "But I never knew she even married. I mean, there were the affairs with her male costars, the rumors, the headlines—but children...?"

"She never married in Hollywood because she never divorced my father. She wasn't free to marry, though he would have given her a divorce any time she wanted it. All she had to do was ask." He continued to stare, bemused, at the ceiling, thoughtfully rubbing his jaw. "Dad was an Irish horse trainer. Mom was Mexican. He married her when she was sixteen. Dad never tried to make any mileage locally out of the fact that Savanna Black was his wife. Not many people connected Conchita Sanchez, the pretty little runaway Mexican wife of Sean Cassidy, to the ravishing beauty in Hollywood." He turned his eyes to Gina. "Funny thing about my mother—she wasn't only beautiful, she was a great actress. You don't often get that combination. I mean, you get great actresses who are attractive, even beautiful, but my mother had that sex appeal that just exploded off the screen." He frowned. "It's too bad she had to die. She would have just been pushing fifty now."

"Did you ever visit her while you were in Hollywood?"

Colin chuckled ironically. "Never. I went to Hollywood, but when she found out I was there, she never seemed to have any time to see me. A couple of occasions we had appointments to meet, but she always ended up canceling. They were legitimate excuses, I'll give her that, but still, she never seemed interested in seeing her only son. Maybe she didn't want to be reminded of her life before she hit the Big Time."

Gina's heart ached for him. "Maybe you should have tried harder to see her," she suggested gently. "Maybe she was so busy..."

"*She* left me," Colin snapped. "If she didn't give a damn about her own kid, then I wasn't about to horn in on this great new life she'd made for herself."

"Oh, Colin," Gina said softly, mournfully. Now, suddenly, she felt she was beginning to know him, to understand him. There had been great pain in his life, as she'd suspected, but she hadn't realized just how great it was. He'd been abandoned by his mother at the vulnerable age of six then later found himself attracted to the same kind of women—beautiful, ambitious women. Suddenly Gina started. "Colin?"

"Yes?"

"Sally? What did she look like? All I know is she had brown eyes."

He shrugged. "Dark hair, brown eyes—dark coloring." He shrugged again, then went still. "Oh," he said at last. "Oh, I see. You've made a connection."

It was Gina's time to shrug. "I'm dark," she said. "I'm ambitious."

He stared into space, then nodded. "Yeah, I guess you're right."

"So maybe it isn't so much a case of my looking for a father," Gina said gently, "as your looking for a mother...."

At that, Colin sat up and grabbed her elbow, holding it so tightly Gina almost cried out. "If you think what I feel for you is remotely what a son feels for his mother..." he said threateningly.

"Colin, you're hurting me!"

Stricken, he released her, then raked his hand through his hair. "I'm sorry, I didn't mean to hurt you, Gina, but, by God, if you're implying that I'm looking for maternal affection, you're crazy. These are male hormones that are racing around my body, Longford, and if I weren't afraid you'd accuse me of being overly crude, I'd tell you exactly what I'd like to do right now, in frank, four-letter, Anglo-Saxon terms."

"I didn't mean it that way," Gina said. "I only meant—" She broke off, stumped by what she really *did* mean. "Well, I meant that you've somehow tangled your mother up with your relationships with women. At least that's how it seems to me, but what do I know?" She looked away from his curiously remote eyes and sighed. "I'm sorry, I was just saying what occurred to me. I mean, it's probably more than a coincidence that you're attracted and repelled at the same time to women who are dark and pretty and ambitious."

He was silent a while, then he said, "You're more than pretty, Longford. You're beautiful."

She glanced at him and saw immediately that his mood had changed. He was no longer angry with her. Instead, he seemed almost peaceful, as if finally talking about it had released some of the pent-up pain he'd carried inside for too long.

"You're not angry at me, then," she said.

He shook his head, his eyes filled with a strange, devastating warmth. "No," he said softly, "I'm not angry with you."

She felt a nervous flutter in her stomach and shifted uneasily on the rug. The mood in the room had changed suddenly from the easy camaraderie of the past half hour to something else entirely. Colin was looking at her with slumberous eyes that flickered with admiration. She felt another lurching in the pit of her stomach, felt a strong, hot shaft of desire shoot through her, setting her blood on fire, making her pulses pound. She was suddenly aware that she was clad only in the skimpy beige teddy with its lavish lace trim. Awkwardly she reached out for her robe, but Colin stopped her.

"No," he said softly. "You're not getting away now."

"Who's talking about getting away?" she said nervously. "I was just getting a little cool."

"Then I'll warm you, like I promised a while back."

Gina felt her apprehension grow, expanding like a cloud on the horizon, until it had turned to excitement. Nervous flutters continued to attack her midsection, and warm currents moved voluptuously over her skin, making her tremble with something that wasn't even remotely connected to fear.

"And just exactly how will you warm me?" she asked, her voice suddenly low and throaty.

He brushed the back of his hand across her cheek then pushed her hair back from her face. "I'll think of a way," he whispered.

She shivered again, his touch and nearness affecting her as she'd never been affected. She was hot and cold at the same time, nervous and excited, wanting him to grab her and carry her off to bed, yet wanting his seduction to last all night.

"Perhaps," he murmured, tracing a fingertip down the side of her neck and over her shoulder, dislodging the slender strap of her teddy in the process, "perhaps I'll warm you with just my touch." He trailed his hand down her arm, leaving sensual shivers in its wake.

"Or maybe I'll warm you with kisses." He leaned toward her and brushed his lips across her bare shoulder. "Like this." She lay back, luxuriating in the delight of his touch, shivering as he trailed his lips closer and closer to her satin-covered breast.

"Or like this," he whispered, and began nibbling at the tiny, satin-covered buttons of her teddy. Slowly, one by one, he somehow yanked them open with his teeth, laying bare her firm breasts in the process, exposing them to both the cool air of the room and the blazing heat from the fireplace.

Groaning, he slid the other strap off her shoulder, then parted her teddy, uncovering her breasts with their dusky, aroused nipples. Expectation flowered inside Gina, sending tremulous shivers floating through her.

"Touch me, Colin," she whispered softly. "Please, touch me."

"Ahh, Gina," he said, burying his head between her breasts, "I thought I'd never hear you say those words to me."

She put her arms around him, savoring the feel of his skin against her own, then his hand cupped her left breast and she gasped with delight. His hand was so large it completely engulfed her breast, and his palm was work-rough and calloused, yet he moved with special gentle sensuality over her nipple, massaging in erotic circles, arousing her until she felt on fire with need, lost in a world of sensation.

Then he brushed his lips over her other breast and she gasped again, delighted by the moist laving of his lips and tongue over her aroused nipple while he continued to massage her other yearning, aching breast.

"Oh God," she moaned, eyes closed in rapture, head thrown back, her dark hair forming a wild, unruly nimbus around her. "Oh, it feels so good."

"It'll get better, sweetheart," Colin crooned, nuzzling the hollow of her throat.

"How?" she asked, laughing huskily, arching her back to thrust her breasts into his hands. She moved her upper body in circles, her eyes still closed, her lips parted in rapture as he continued to caress her.

"Oh, please," she groaned.

He dropped his hand gently down her satin-covered tummy until he came to the lace-trimmed bottom of the teddy, teasing her slowly.

Carefully, he inched his fingers beneath the lace edges and found her warmth. She moaned and shivered violently, then moved her body under his questing hand, feeling the incredible surge of heat build up, opening her, making her ready for his invasion.

Slowly, one by one, he unfastened the three tiny clasps at the bottom of her teddy. He parted her legs and rubbed her sensuously, finding the exact spots that gave her the most pleasure, bringing her to the brink of ecstasy, only to take her back. She cried out with mingled desire and frustration, moving her hips gently back and forth, feeling his strong fingers caress her.

Again, she gasped with pleasure, growing almost lightheaded with desire. "Colin," she whispered, "I want you inside me."

He quickly divested himself of his clothing, protected himself and gently lowered himself onto her. The feel of his naked body against hers brought new shivers of delight, and she wound her arms around him and opened her legs to his invasion.

When it came, it was so beautiful it took her breath away, as if his very soul were enveloping her. He buried himself inside her even as she opened and flowered, gliding in and out in a strong, pulsing rhythm.

And the more he plunged into her, then withdrew, the deeper he plunged the next time, until the beauty built inside her, leaving her breathless with wonderment, whimpering with joy that mingled with something remotely like pain.

"Oh, yes!" she breathed, feeling the waves begin to build inside her. "Yes, Colin."

"Gina," he whispered. "Let it happen, my beautiful darling."

His loving words sent her spilling over the edge, floating and cascading into a waterfall of glory.

They stayed nestled close together as the flames slowly died in the fireplace, warming each other with their body heat, occasionally slipping into slumber, then coming awake to make slow, languorous love again.

It was near dawn when the idyll ended. Gina awakened to the unaccustomed sound of silence. Turning, she looked into Colin's eyes.

"It's stopped raining," he said.

She felt her heart fall with disappointment. As long as they'd had the rain, they'd had each other. Now, Colin would have to leave. Now, when she'd found what she truly wanted, it was going to end. She turned wide eyes to him and reached for him hungrily. "Hold me," she whispered. "Hold me, Colin, and then make love to me."

It was the only way she knew to cope with the knowledge that in a few hours, he could be gone, out of her life forever, except as a remote working partner on a syndicated television program.

Ten
───

Cut!'' yelled Peter Davis, the director of *Hollywood Report Card*, Gina's and Colin's new television program. "That was good, but I'd like you two to relax a little. You both seem afraid of really letting go and saying what you feel. Remember how it was in your audition? You went at each other like tigers. Today you were a little too polite. It's okay to be this way when you agree with each other, but for crying out loud, when you disagree, go for the jugular once in a while! That's what we hired you for!''

Gina glanced at Colin then looked away quickly. They'd been taping for hours and yet she knew something was wrong. They couldn't seem to attain their old animosity. Instead, there was a feeling of discomfort between them, as if they were two strangers who'd been thrown together and didn't have a clue how to work together. But it was only their first day of taping. Perhaps it would take a while for them to get the hang of it.

"How about taking a break?" Peter suggested. "Then we'll start over in fifteen minutes."

Gina stood up, arching her back to get the kinks out, then she glanced at Colin, but he refused to look at her. Instead, he turned and walked away, heading out of the taping studio down the hall toward the coffee machine.

For a moment, Gina was hurt at his ignoring her, then her temper began to sizzle. Just who did he think he was? Granted they'd shared what was commonly known as a one-night stand, but couldn't he have the common decency to at least be courteous to her? That would be the decent thing to do, but then why had she ever conceived the idea that Colin could be decent?

Feeling more and more angry, Gina began to pace the set, her green eyes sparkling dangerously, her high heels tapping a rhythm on the floor's tiled surface.

"Upset at something, Gina?" Colin asked from behind her.

Startled, she whirled around to find him lounging against the wall, a cup of coffee in one hand, a knowing smile on his arrogant face. "No," she snapped. "Why should I be? I knew this program wouldn't work from the start. Today's taping only proves it."

"Oh, so it's the taping that's bothering you," he said, sipping his coffee unconcernedly.

"I didn't say that!" Gina said heatedly. "I said nothing's bothering me!"

"Sure seems to be something bothering you," he said, yawning. "For a while there, I wondered if you were mad because I haven't seen you since I left your place a week ago."

Gina laughed scornfully. "Now why on earth would *that* bother me? Honestly, Colin, you'd think I actually *cared* for you or something. I assure you, I'm a thoroughly modern woman. One-night stands aren't cause for tears anymore, Cassidy. Most women are as glad when the man leaves as he is."

"I see." Colin gazed at her from over the rim of his coffee cup, his dark eyes taunting, telling her he knew she was putting up a front that didn't convince him in the least.

Furious, Gina whirled on her heel and stomped back to the set. "Well?" she said irritably, "are we going to tape today or sit around and cool our heels all day?"

Peter Davis looked up from the script and raised his eyebrows. "You sound upset, Gina. Anything wrong?"

She threw her hands up. "Why is everyone asking me if something's wrong?" she demanded hotly. "Nothing's wrong, okay?" She folded her arms and began to pace back and forth. "Well, nothing's wrong other than a headache the size of the Grand Canyon and a show that looks like a cross between Mr. Rogers and Howdy Doody."

"You aren't pleased with the taping so far, Gina?" Peter asked cautiously, his eyes gleaming with interest.

"No, I am *not* pleased," she stormed. "It stinks, to put it bluntly. That charisma you thought Colin and I had is about as exciting as a deflated balloon the day after a parade."

"Now, Gina," Peter said placatingly, "it's not all that bad. You two are just starting. Quite often it takes a few shows for two people to form a partnership and start working well together."

"Well, we don't have a few shows, Peter, and you know it. The network's holding an ax over our heads. We're up against some other movie review programs as it is. This one has to be special, and so far it's about as special as the corned beef and cabbage at Paddy Martin's on Saturday night."

"What do you think, Colin?" Peter asked, turning to Colin who still lazed against the back wall.

"I think you were right the first time. I think Gina's just as grumpy as an old mule."

Gina's eyes took fire. She turned to face him slowly, her head high, her hand on her hip. "From now on, Cassidy," she said acidly, "if you're asked for an opinion, make it constructive, okay? We don't need your so-called witticisms muddying the waters here."

"Speaking of muddy water, how's your driveway, Gina?" Colin asked, sauntering by as he headed for his chair on the set.

She almost flinched, knowing he was referring to what had occurred between them in a roundabout way. "It's fine," she said coolly. "Which is more than I can say for you."

"Hey, you two," Peter said, rubbing his hands together enthusiastically, "let's bury the hatchet, okay? It's beginning to sound like you two don't much like each other."

"Like each other?" Gina echoed, then laughed scornfully. "Peter, liking each other wasn't part of the deal, if you remember correctly, so stop being such a hypocrite and let's get taping."

Peter looked momentarily stunned then glanced at Colin, who simply shrugged with an "I told you so" look on his face. Seeing the exchange between the two men set Gina's teeth on edge. She'd never behaved this abominably, but she couldn't seem to help herself. It had to be caused by Colin's presence. He acted on her like a match on gunpowder.

"I'm sorry, Peter," she mumbled, rubbing the back of her neck. "I really do have a beast of a headache. I guess I'm a little stressed out."

"Mmm," murmured Colin complacently. "The muscles in the back of Gina's neck really get tense when she's upset."

Peter peered over his spectacles at Colin, then he glanced at Gina speculatively. "Oh?" he said noncommittally, then went back to the script. But the unasked question—How would you know?—seemed to hang in the air, causing Gina to blush beet-red. She gave Colin an irritable look and took her seat opposite him. "That really wasn't necessary," she said to him under her breath.

"Did I say something wrong?" Colin asked innocently.

She smiled acidly, but refrained from answering.

"Okay, you two," yelled Peter, "let's get cracking. Take Fifteen!"

"*Gravediggers, Part V* is out," Gina said into the camera, "and folks, it's simply abominable. Both Colin and I agreed that the original *Gravediggers* was a nice twist on the routine bloodbath/teenage-splatter film, but the director of *Part V* has hit a new low. There's no plot, no script, and worst of all, no new special effects. It's the same old ghosts-jumping-from-the-grave routine and teenagers who haven't got the sense to stay away from the cemetery. Martin Polaris, the director, must think all people under twenty are brain dead, because his story line, if you can call it that, reflects a view of teenagers that's so negative, so derogatory and so unflattering, that if I fell in that category, I'd picket the film out of sheer rebellion. For my money, it gets a big red F. It flunks, plain and simple." She turned to Colin, who was slumped in his chair, studying her over steepled fingers.

"Wrong again, Longford," he said lazily. "I agree that parts *II* through *IV* were bad, but in *Part V*, Polaris takes a few risks and manages to salvage most of the movie—"

"Risks?" Gina interrupted, genuinely surprised. "What risks? He hired the same ghouls to come in and claw their way out of the graves, and you call it taking risks?"

"First of all, Gina," Colin said wearily, sounding as if he were getting tired of telling her what was *really* going on in the movies, "it's risky enough just putting another *Gravediggers* out. For courage alone, Polaris has to be credited. Secondly, the special effects *have* changed, contrary to what you said. That one scene at the end was really scary, and he's found a new technique to pull it off. That alone saved the movie for me, so I give it a barely passing grade of D."

"Oh, come on, Colin," Gina remonstrated, "you're judging the movie on technical effects that the average moviegoer doesn't know the least thing about and cares about even less. Is it or is it not worth six bucks on a Saturday night?"

"Not six bucks," admitted Colin, "but I'd sure recommend it when it hits the second-run houses and goes for ninety-nine cents. And it's a sure bet for the home video hit parade."

"Okay," Gina said, "so skip it in its first run, folks, and if you're into ghoul and guts, catch it at home on the VCR." She turned to face another camera and rolled smoothly into her next review. "But let's talk about a real movie for a change. Roger Conover's new movie is a delight...."

"Cut!" Peter yelled exuberantly hours later, then ran up to Gina and Colin and took their hands, shaking them, patting them excitedly, giving Gina a big kiss and slapping Colin on the back. "That's *it*! It's in the can! You *did* it! My God, it was great. Compared to this morning's work, you two sizzled on camera. For a first show, we've got a winner. You started out well with the *Gravediggers* review and went straight uphill from there, pulling out all the stops and really getting down and dirty. The viewers are gonna love you guys!" He clapped Colin on the back again, hugged Gina, then went trotting off, waving his script excitedly and calling for the film editor to follow him.

Gina stared wearily after him then slumped into her chair and began to knead the muscles at the back of her neck.

"You really have a headache?" Colin asked from beside her.

She made a face at him. "No," she said ironically, "I feel like Muhammad Ali at his first title defense, fighting and raring to go."

"No need to snap at me anymore, Gina, we're off camera."

She eyed him sourly then heaved herself from the chair. "It wasn't an act for the camera, Cassidy," she said. "Now if you don't mind, I'm going home and taking an hour-long soak in the tub. I feel rotten. See you next week."

She grabbed her coat from a nearby chair and threw it over her shoulders, then walked slowly down the empty hall toward the door to the parking lot. The network had decided to tape the shows at their New Haven affiliate, for which she was eternally thankful. She was still able to work at the paper in Hartford and tape the show one day a week. It also meant she could be home in half an hour and in that tub.

But when she got home, she slumped onto the living room couch and stared glumly at the fireplace. She hadn't lit it once since the night over a week ago when she and Colin had made love in front of it. Somehow, she couldn't bring herself to, feeling as if the flames wouldn't be as bright or warm without Colin's presence.

Now, she sniffed at herself in derision. What a fool she'd been. Couldn't she face the fact that Colin Cassidy had completely fooled her? She'd thought he was changing, "opening up," when all along, he'd simply loaded the hook with the bait he knew would work on her—the simple, sincere, honest approach. She gritted her teeth and emitted a low groan, then started when a pounding sounded on her front door.

Puzzled at who might be calling at this hour, she went to the door and peered out the peephole. What she saw set her teeth on edge. Of all the nerve! Colin Cassidy stood facing her, a big grin on his face, holding up two bags from a fast-food chain.

She ripped open the door. "What do you want?" she demanded.

"My, my," Colin said mildly, stepping around her and kicking the front door shut, "aren't you the gracious hostess?"

"I wasn't aware I *was* a hostess," she countered. "Who issued the invitation, pray tell?"

"I issued it myself," Colin said, taking her hand and pulling her reluctant body behind him into the living room. "Want to light a fire?"

"No!" Gina shouted.

Taken aback, Colin turned and stared at her a minute then shrugged. "Okay, no problem. What do you want?" he asked, opening one of the bags, "Super Burger or a simple cheeseburger with onions?"

"What I *want*," Gina said in exasperation, "is for you to leave. And please take that...that...*junk* food with you."

"Now, Gina," Colin said in a reasonable tone, "you said you were tired and had a headache. I thought I was being a friend to do this. I knew you wouldn't feel like getting your own dinner."

"Okay," she said, putting a hand on her hip and leaning on the couch with her other hand, "what do you really want? Out with it, Cassidy. I'm not in the mood for your little games.''

"Games?" Colin echoed innocently. "What do you mean by that?''

"What I mean," Gina said, "is that you purposely ignored me today during the taping. You were rude and acted like a complete boor. After what happened between us—" She stopped fast, feeling her cheeks begin to flush, then forced herself to go on. "What I mean is, after what *occurred* between us, your behavior was particularly reprehensible. The least we can do is act like two adults, admit it was a case of overstimulated glands that turned into a big mistake, and be courteous to each other. But no, you have to act as if I were a leper. I almost expected you to pull out a bell and ask me to ring it whenever I approached."

Colin sat on the edge of the arm of the couch and began chomping on the cheeseburger. "It really worked, didn't it?" he asked, reaching for a french fry and chocolate milk shake.

"What worked?" Gina asked, staring at him with repulsion as he practically inhaled one cheeseburger and unwrapped another.

"My act," he answered unconcernedly.

"Your *act*?"

"Yeah." Colin looked up from his milk shake. "I could see we were so uncomfortable with each other after what happened that we weren't working well together, so I decided to get your dander up. I knew if you got angry, things would be okay between us." He grinned at her. "So, do I get a kiss for being a genius now or after we go to bed?"

His final words flustered her so much that she began to stammer, trying to decide if she were angry or elated. She decided she was angry. Anger with Colin always seemed to work the best. "You cad," she said in a low, shaking voice. "You lowlife—"

"Get to the point, Gina," Colin said amiably. "Here, you want this Super Burger, 'cause if you don't, I'm eating it."

"Go ahead and eat it!" Gina yelled, then took a deep breath and began to walk around the room. "I can't believe you have the audacity to come waltzing in here, expecting to go to bed with me when you haven't even called me, not even once, since the first time. What am I? The local floozy? You think once gives you the right to expect a second time?"

Colin sat on the edge of the couch, staring at her thoughtfully as he chewed. "Answer me this," he said finally, "what makes a phone call so damned important to a woman? I've never understood it."

"What makes a phone call—?" Gina broke off in frustration. How could a man *not* understand? It was as simple as elementary education—a woman needed to be reassured that it hadn't been just sex, that the man was really interested in her, that she hadn't been used.

She groaned and sat down on the raised hearth and began kneading her temples. "Oh, Lord," she moaned, "I've got the worst headache of my life. Will you please just leave?"

"Where's the aspirin?" Colin asked, getting up and heading for the hall.

"Medicine cabinet, top-right shelf," Gina said automatically. The pounding in her head was so intense she wondered if she would ever get rid of it. Was this what they called a migraine?

Colin was back quickly, holding out two aspirin and a glass of water. "Take them," he ordered.

She obeyed without argument, knowing that what he commanded made sense. She drained the glass and set it down on the hearth with a sigh. "Why don't you put me out of my misery and leave?" she finally asked. "This headache is all your doing."

"Then I'll have to be responsible for getting rid of it, won't I?"

She looked up at him with exasperation. "No, Colin, it doesn't work that way. It's not like the Indians, who were forever responsible for you if you saved their lives. Now will you kindly leave?"

"No," Colin said, walking behind her and beginning to knead the muscles at the top of her shoulders.

The massage felt so good, Gina almost groaned, but caught herself in time. "Colin, leave."

"No." He continued to knead her muscles, running his thumbs up her neck, then down, then using all ten fingers to knead away the tension at the tops of her shoulders. "That's right," he crooned softly, "just relax."

She did. She couldn't help it. The massage felt so wonderful she felt as if she were melting. Finally, she couldn't hold it back, and she gave a low groan of pleasure.

"Was that pleasure or pain?" Colin asked.

"Pleasure."

"Good."

She tried to think of a retort, but none came. She was too busy glorying in the feel of his strong hands kneading out the kinks one by one. Finally she couldn't hold it back any longer. "Oh, God. That feels so wonderful."

"You're feeling better then?"

She nodded, her eyes closed, a rapt smile on her face.

"Good. Wait right there and don't move while I run a bath for you."

"A bath?" she said in amazement, then just stretched out on the carpet and closed her eyes. Lord, how good it felt to have someone take care of her for once. Such an unaccustomed luxury! In the entire two years of her marriage, she didn't think Jack had once given her a back rub, brought her an aspirin or run her a hot bath.

"Okay," Colin said, reappearing. "It's almost ready for you."

"Mmm," she murmured, eyes still closed. "Sounds wonderful."

Colin put his hands on his hips and stared down at her, grinning. "You don't look like you're capable of moving."

"For a hot bath, I'll give it a try," she said, struggling to sit up.

"No need," Colin said gently, reaching down and gathering her in his arms.

"What are you—?" Gina threw her arms around Colin and held on tightly, so taken by surprise that she felt momentarily disoriented.

"I'm carrying you, what does it feel like?" Colin said softly.

"Oh." She was so exhausted, she simply put her head on his shoulder and gave herself up to the exquisite pleasure of being carried. She'd never been carried in her life before she met Colin, maybe because she looked so damn capable, maybe because she hadn't until now met a man who understood that every woman on earth wanted to be carried at least once in her life, if only to confirm the fact that she didn't weigh so much that it was an impossible feat for the man.

The bathroom was filled with fragrant steam when Colin kicked open the door, and the water was almost to the top of the tub. A thick pile of bubbles floated on the water's surface, like meringue on a lemon pie. Carefully Colin undressed her, then helped her into the tub.

"You okay?" he asked. "Can you sit down by yourself or are you going to slip and crack your head open?"

She smiled dazedly and sat down, sinking into the heated water with a drawn-out sigh of rapture. "Oh, God," she whispered, closing her eyes and leaning her head back on the rim of the tub. "I would have killed for this."

"And you didn't have to raise a finger," Colin said, perching on the edge of the tub and watching her.

She opened one eye and peered up at him. "Why?" was all she asked.

"What?"

"You heard me."

He shrugged. "You truly looked beat. I wanted to. Who knows? I did it, that's all that matters."

She nodded gratefully and closed her eyes again. "You've performed a miracle," she said. "My headache's gone and I feel three-hundred-percent better."

"Good," Colin said. "Does that mean I get to stay the night?"

His question took her completely by surprise. She opened her eyes slowly and stared at him. Should she or shouldn't she? She met his gaze squarely, weighing the consequences, then she realized that she loved the way he looked right now, with his hair slightly tousled and his beard beginning to show, and his shirt wrinkled.

Then she realized something else: she wanted him, as much as she'd wanted him that first night, and probably even more. She heaved a delicate sigh and lifted her shoulders in a helpless shrug. "Why not?" she said lightly. "We *are* partners, after all...."

Eleven

Gina giggled in delight, looking down into Colin's eyes as she straddled him, her glorious hair forming a rich curtain around them, shutting out the invading rays of the morning sun.

"You're cooking breakfast, Mr. Cassidy," she said again. "And that's final."

"I told you, Gina," Colin protested. "I can't cook."

"Then all the more reason to cook this morning—it's time for you to learn. We'll call it the Life Survival Skills Course, Part One—The Nutritious Morning Breakfast."

He rolled over and trapped her under his large body, chuckling as he nuzzled the dusky peaks of her breasts. "I'd rather stay here with you. You're more nutritious than any old breakfast."

Gina's breath caught in her lungs as the familiar whirlwind of desire began to churn in her midsection. "Colin," she whispered pleadingly, "don't."

"But you like it," he murmured, licking her nipple, then tugging softly on it with his teeth.

Again her breath shook in her lungs and her eyes took on a rapt expression of delight. "But we can't stay in bed all morning...."

"Why can't we? Any law against it?"

She laughed huskily and ran her forefinger down his cheek, staring up into his face with glowing eyes. It had been a night she would never forget, a night of love so perfect, so wonderful, just thinking about it set her blood on fire. Colin was a masterful lover—gentle, considerate, loving, yet entirely romantic and uninhibited, freeing her naturally passionate nature so that she not only received pleasure but gave it, too.

If only they could learn to work this way together out of bed. If only they could learn to give to each other, to care for each other in as loving a way as they had last night. If they could, she thought they would make a perfect couple.

She sighed and rolled out from under Colin and sat up, staring dreamily out the windows, where the autumn sun blazed in a perfect blue sky. Colin reached out and began rubbing her back.

"Hey, pretty," he said softly. "You really want me to cook this morning?"

She turned around and met his gaze. "It'd be nice," she said wryly, "kinda like a fairy tale come true, but I guess I can put up with pouring cereal and milk into two bowls." She smiled impishly, leaping out of bed. "You can wash dishes!"

"Hey!" he yelled in protest. "I hate washing dishes!"

She slipped into a lacy bra and bikini panties, then pulled on a pair of faded jeans and a zip-up sweatshirt. "Those are the breaks, Cassidy. In this house, everyone contributes. You cook or you clean. You made your choice, now live with it.'' With that, she flounced into the bathroom and slammed the door behind her, grinning to herself as she listened to Colin grumbling in the bedroom as he dressed. When the bedroom door slammed on a low curse, her grin faded and she leaned against the bathroom sink, staring down at the strip of toothpaste on her toothbrush.

Dammit, why did she always have to fall for macho men? Why couldn't she meet some nice liberated guy who understood that women got *tired*? Women were expected to clean the house, hold down a demanding job—in her case two demanding jobs—the newspaper column and the television show—and then they were expected to be as sexy and explosive as a stick of dynamite in bed.

Yet she had to hand it to Colin—last night he'd been as loving and considerate as any man she'd ever dreamed about. He'd brought her dinner, even if it *was* a Super Burger that he ended up eating, then he'd taken care of her, bringing her aspirin for her headache, giving her a massage, drawing her a bath, then making slow, wonderful love to her.

She sighed again and headed for the kitchen, then came to a stop in the living room. Two bags from the local hamburger joint littered the floor, along with the cheeseburger and Super Burger wrappings and two little aluminum foil packets of catsup and mustard. Gina stared at them then sank into a chair, feeling dismay overwhelm her.

Was it like this for every woman on earth? Did she have to settle for a genuine slob to get a wonderful lover? Was she asking too much? Had finding a man who contributed to cleaning the house become so important that she was missing the essential meaning of shared love? Perhaps this was the way it had to be—the woman doing all the work, eternally picking up after a man, emptying his ashtrays, wash-

ing his dirty socks and underwear, cooking and cleaning and
tidying—

The door from the kitchen swung open and Colin appeared in the doorway. "Well?" he asked, sounding oddly irritable. "We having breakfast this morning or what?"

Gina's fingers curled around the edges of the arms of the chair, but she bit back the natural retort that came to her lips. She took a deep breath and stood up, then slowly began picking up the litter in the living room.

"I'll be right there, Colin," she said quietly. "I just want to straighten up in here first."

Without a word, he let the kitchen door swing shut and immediately Gina slumped onto the couch, clutching the cheeseburger wrappers and the aluminum foil packages of catsup and mustard. She stuffed them in one of the bags, feeling dismay and disappointment flow through her, as rough and stormy as a river after a flood.

It was no use. It wouldn't work. She couldn't do *everything.* There had to be some sort of sharing in a relationship. Fifty years ago, it had made sense that the woman cooked and cleaned while the man worked outside the house, but things were different today. Nowadays, women worked outside the home, too, and yet they were still stuck with keeping house and taking care of children and running the errands and—

Gina sat back and closed her eyes, feeling exhaustion wash over her in a giant wave. She couldn't keep fighting it, couldn't keep up this everlasting battle with the men in her life. Physical attraction and wonderful lovemaking were terrific, but there was more to life than good sex. Gina felt as if she would be turning her back on herself and her own needs, her own *rights*, if she gave in to Colin and let him sweet talk his way into her bed while refusing to be considerate in any other way.

Tiredly, she dragged herself from the couch, preparing to enter the kitchen and do battle. Except it wouldn't be just one battle, it would be the final one. She would tell him she couldn't ever see him again outside the studio. She would try to explain, in as loving a way as she could, that she just couldn't do it all. She wasn't Superwoman, she was just plain old Gina Longford, frail human being.

She pushed open the kitchen door and came to a stop, stunned. Two bowls of cereal were set out on the kitchen table, with a carton of milk set in the middle of the table next to two banana peels, obviously discarded after Colin had cut the bananas into quarters and laid them crisscross atop the cereal. She stared at the bananas, then lifted bemused eyes to Colin, who was sitting watching her, a defensive look on his face.

"Well?" he said crankily, "what do you think? I made breakfast."

She felt all her earlier misgivings melt, replaced by a feeling of such love and tenderness that she knew until this very moment, she'd never really loved anyone before, not really. There were flakes of cereal littering the table, and the box was still open on the counter, and the banana peels were absolutely disgusting-looking, and the way he'd cut the bananas—quartering them instead of slicing them, as if a gorilla and not a human were going to eat them—none of this mattered. All that mattered was that he'd *tried*. Clumsy, awkward, messy, his efforts were as beautiful to Gina as the finest service in the best New York restaurant.

"Oh, Colin," she said softly, hugging the hamburger wrappings to her breasts, her eyes misting with tears. "Oh, Colin, this is . . . why it's just perfect."

He looked down at the messy table. "Well, it really wasn't all that hard. I don't know why you women are constantly complaining about cooking and preparing meals. This was a snap."

Her smile froze on her face. "What did you say?" she asked carefully. Her fingers tightened on the hamburger wrappings as she considered throwing them at him.

"This," he said, gesturing at the mess around him, "it was easy. I could do this every morning."

"I'll bet you could," she said sweetly, lobbing the hamburger litter in the wastebasket with a perfect hook shot.

Colin slowly sat back. "Okay, what'd I do? You were pleased at first. I saw your face—you looked like you were going to throw your arms around me and kiss me. What'd I say that ruined it for you?"

She shrugged innocently and sat down, taking a knife and beginning to cut the quartered banana into neat circles atop her cereal. Then she began to sweep up the cereal flakes that littered the tabletop, deposited them in the garbage, got out a pitcher and poured the milk into it, returned the milk carton to the refrigerator, then sat down and began to eat.

"Oh, I get it," Colin said darkly. "It wasn't good enough for you. Everything has to be perfect for Gina Longford, is that it?"

Stricken, she looked up at him, her eyes wide. "It *was* perfect," she whispered shakily. "It was the most beautiful, thoughtful, wonderful thing you could have done for me—except for last night, when you were so wonderful to me—but..." She looked down, blinking back sudden tears. "It was what you *said*, Colin."

"What'd I say?" he asked. "I said it was easy. I said I could do it. I said anyone could do it and I meant it."

Her fingers trembled as she picked up her spoon and dipped it in the cereal. What was there to say? She was back at the same impasse, wondering why there was such an unbridgeable gulf between men and women. They were all human beings, weren't they? Both sexes had eyes, both had ears. Why then did they see things so differently, hear things that were never said, never meant?

"Gina," Colin said, "please look at me."

She hesitated, then slowly lifted her eyes to his, all her misery and confusion mirrored in her gaze. "I'm sorry," she murmured softly. "I really did appreciate what you've done. I *do* appreciate it! I really do, Colin." She forced a sad smile. "It was wonderful of you to do this for me."

"So what's the problem, Gina?"

She lifted her hands helplessly then let them fall. "I don't know," she said miserably, "it was just that when you said it was so easy, it sounded like you thought it *is* easy to do everything, and it *isn't*, Colin, it just isn't! Sometimes I want to close the door on this place, as much as I love it, and never come home. I want to get in my car and just ride west into the sunset and never look at another dust cloth or can opener or cleanser. The thing about cooking and cleaning and housework is, it never *ends*, Colin. The minute you clean up after one meal, it's time to start on the next. After a while, you begin to feel like a slave to the house."

She took a deep breath to calm down, then continued. "You're right—one meal *is* easy. One of anything is easy. It's the constant repetition that gets to you. It's like Chinese water torture—the constant drip-drip-drip of housework. It never ends. Never. And you begin to resent it, until finally you think you'll scream if you see one more dirty dish or dust kitty."

"Dust kitty?"

She almost laughed at the look of complete bewilderment on his face. "You know," she said, waving at the floor, "those little balls of dust that blow around in the breeze if you haven't swept in a week."

"Well, they don't *hurt* anyone, do they?" Colin asked. "I mean, you could just let them blow around until they piled up, then do one good cleaning and you'd be done with them for another month."

Gina put her elbow on the table and let her chin sink into her hand and stared at Colin, completely bemused. "You think differently from women, that's it. Men think differently. It's a left-brain, right-brain thing. It has to be."

Colin sighed in frustration, ran a hand through his hair, then sat back. "Explain yourself."

"I can't."

"Try."

She took a breath, then tried: "Okay. Look. You buy a house, right?" Colin nodded. "And then you buy furniture?" Again, he nodded. "Okay," she continued, "so you've got this investment, see? And you want to keep it up, not let it deteriorate. So you clean, because if you let things go, there's this cruddy stuff called wax buildup and dirt buildup and the furniture starts to get scratched and the floors begin to get dull and ants get in and start eating your food in the pantry, and then a hairline crack in the ceiling gets wider and before you know it, winter arrives and you're in the middle of a blizzard and the snow's thicker in the house than it is outside."

She sighed mightily, tired from just thinking about it all. "You see, it all comes down to *responsibility*, Colin. And we women know that someone has to be responsible. We look around and see the dirt and the grease and the rotten banana peels and we know *someone* has to do it. But if we left it to men, it'd never get done, and pretty soon we'd be living in a pigsty and there'd go our investment, right down the tubes.

"So we do it, but all the while, we're really *angry* inside, you know? Because it's all on *us*. Because even if the man sees it and hates the mess, he won't lift a finger, because it never once occurs to him that it's a shared responsibility. He grows up thinking it's the woman's job, and it never once hits him that it isn't written in a Book of Gold up in heaven that Woman Shall Clean; Man Shall Lie Down and Watch Television.''

Colin sat with his arms folded and his lips pursed, staring at her from under dark brows. ''Now you want to hear our side of it?''

She shrugged. ''Sure.''

''It *is* kind of like an investment,'' he agreed, ''but we figure we put out the money, so why should we be the ones to keep it up? It's all a matter of division of labor.''

Dumbfounded, Gina stared. ''I don't believe you said that.''

Colin ran a hand down his face and sighed raggedly. ''Okay, so I put it badly. But the division of labor thing applies, you have to admit that.''

''I don't have to admit it,'' she said firmly, her eyes flashing.

''I see.'' He looked around, then shrugged. ''Gina, there *are* guys who cook and clean, you know.''

''I know.''

''I'm just not one of them.''

She tapped a fingernail on the kitchen table but didn't say anything, just sat patiently, waiting.

''Look,'' he said, holding up his hands. ''Admit one thing: I came in here and I made breakfast.''

''You did,'' she said, feeling her anger dissipate at the memory. ''And I think it's terrific. I truly appreciate it, and—''

''And?''

She sat there, looking at him with eyes filled with warmth, and she realized that she was caught: she was falling in love with him. She would put up with him, with his messy ways, his slob tendencies, his utterly chauvinistic attitude, because she cared about him. But she wasn't going to stop fighting. It would be an uphill battle, but she would wage it or go down trying. "And I think this is a wonderful first step," she finished.

"First step?" He looked around, a doubtful expression on his face. "I thought it would do as an only step."

She shook her head.

He sighed and folded his arms and sat back, eyeing her sardonically. "Is this what they call the battle of the sexes?"

"I guess so," she said, shrugging.

"I don't think I like it."

"Neither do I," she said, lifting her shoulders helplessly, "but there you have it."

"You're a hard woman, Gina Longford."

"I'm an insistent one," she amended. "A realistic one. I'm no patsy, Cassidy. I ain't gonna roll over and purr just because I like the way you make love. If you think I'm suddenly going to bow and scrape and ask how you like your eggs every morning, you're in for a rude awakening."

"I suppose you expect *me* to ask how you like *your* eggs every morning," he said sarcastically.

A slow smile edged onto her face. "No-o," she said slowly. "It's more like, I cook one morning, and you clean, then I clean the next morning and you cook. It's called shared responsibility, Colin."

He scratched his chin and ruminated on that. "What other possibilities are there?"

"You could leave and never come back."

He eyed her ruefully. "You're determined, aren't you, lady?"

"Yes."

"No nonsense. No compromises."

"Oh, now wait a minute," she protested. "There are plenty of compromises! That's what it's all about—compromise. We're a *team*, Cassidy. Partners. Get it? That means we work *together*. We can work as a team solely in front of the cameras, or we could..."

"We could what, Longford?" he asked, his eyes narrowing.

She shrugged. "We could...sort of...live together, or something." She glanced quickly at him, then looked away, pretending to be unconcerned with his reaction. "I mean, you're having a hard time finding a place to stay, aren't you?"

He fiddled with his spoon, his expression unreadable. "I haven't seen anything that's impressed me so far, that's true, but I've only been looking for a week."

"You told me you've looked at fifteen places this week," Gina said, examining her nails. "That doesn't sound too promising."

Colin sat back, his eyes narrowed thoughtfully. "It sounds as if you're offering me a deal: I can stay here with you under one condition—that I help out around the place."

"You catch on fast, Cassidy," she said. "You're a real quick study. Why, I bet you'll take to doing washes and folding clothes in no time. Not to mention vacuuming and dusting and scrubbing toilets."

"Toilets!" He held up a hand, shaking his head. "No way, Longford, I draw the line at toilets."

She shrugged and spread her hands helplessly. "Good luck finding that bachelor pad, then, Cassidy." Pushing back her chair, she stood up and began to tidy the kitchen, humming softly under her breath.

"Longford."

Feigning surprise that he was still there, she looked over her shoulder and raised her eyebrows. "Yes?"

"I don't do toilets."

She leaned against the counter, her brow furrowed in pretended concentration. "Which means I have to do them all the time. I don't know, Cassidy," she said slowly, "that sounds a bit like uneven distribution of labor."

"Okay, what about if I did the tub and you did the toilet?"

Gina did her best to hold back a winning grin. Poor man, he was just a neophyte. He didn't know that scrubbing a tub was infinitely harder work than cleaning a silly toilet, especially when it was a huge old claw-footed tub.

"We-ell," she said reluctantly, "you drive an awfully hard bargain...."

He relaxed, as if sensing victory. "I don't know," he said, sounding almost bored. "I suppose we could give it a try. The nights alone would be worth it."

"Only nights?" she asked, widening her eyes innocently.

His dark eyes grew darker. He looked around the kitchen then took her hand and strode toward the door. "Cleaning can wait, just remember that, Gina. Our first and foremost rule is, cleaning can always wait. Lovemaking comes first."

In response, she pulled him to a stop and wound her arms around his neck and began nibbling at his ear. "I like your priorities, Mr. Cassidy," she whispered throatily.

He opened the bedroom door then stood looking into her eyes, his face serious, his voice quiet. "And I like you."

She felt her heart lurch unexpectedly at the sincerity in his tone and knew that something momentous had happened, almost without her even noticing. In a matter of minutes, she and Colin had negotiated a contract: he was going to move in and live with her. Suddenly, she was in a relationship.

"Oh, Colin," she breathed, her eyes shining. "I like you, too."

"Just don't get any funny ideas, Longford," he said, beginning to unbutton his shirt. "This is probably the biggest mistake of your life. I'm not an easy man to live with. You already know I'm a slob. Well, I'm also moody, and I snore sometimes, so any time you want to boot me out, just do it."

Gina cocked her head and stared at him. "You're the biggest pessimist I've ever met," she said softly. "You go out and look for trouble, don't you, Cassidy?"

"It's not pessimism, it's realism," he said, stripping off his shirt and beginning to unbuckle his belt. "I'm a pretty good judge of myself, Longford. My record doesn't exactly make me a winner. You'd probably be smart to tell me to get the hell out now, before we completely ruin even our working relationship."

"You're really afraid of involvement, aren't you, Cassidy?" she asked, eyeing him quizzically. "Don't you realize that your attitude sets up a self-fulfilling prophecy? If you think you'll fail, you will." She shook her head and began to unzip her sweatshirt. "But I don't think we'll fail. I think we'll get along just fine."

Colin's eyes grew darker as he watched her begin to undress slowly. "In the bedroom," he said quietly, "I quite agree with you. Otherwise, I predict it won't work. We're not right for each other. Any fool can see that."

She stared at him a moment, then zipped up her sweatshirt and bent to pick up her nightgown and fold it neatly. "You're just getting cold feet," she said, throwing him a long-suffering glance and beginning to take everything off her dresser.

"What are you doing?" he asked irritably.

"Dusting."

He raised his eyebrows and watched as she whipped out a dust cloth from a closet and polished the dresser top to a fine mirrorlike sheen then dusted every item and replaced each carefully on the top. "I thought we just agreed that lovemaking was our first priority," Colin said.

She cast him a dark look and began rearranging drawers. "Gina."

She didn't respond. She kept her head buried in her underwear drawer, carefully refolding her already perfectly folded bras and panties.

Colin sighed loudly and sat on the edge of the bed. "Okay, let's talk."

"About what?" she asked briskly, shutting a drawer and opening another.

"Us."

"What about us?"

Colin got off the bed and took her arm, turning her to face him. "All right, I admit I'm afraid of getting involved, but it looks to me like you're more scared than I am."

"I'm not scared," she said. "I'm angry. I'm absolutely livid that you have this attitude that you're going to fail at everything you do."

"When a guy's got a record as bad as mine, he has a right to be wary of trying again."

She rubbed her head wearily. "Look, I'm worried, too, okay? I'm wondering if we can weather it, Cassidy," she said softly. "Maybe all we've got going for us is good sex."

"Well, I guess we'll find out, won't we?" he said shortly.

"That's what I'm afraid of."

Looking contrite, he took her in his arms and rocked her back and forth, his chin resting on her head, his eyes troubled. "I won't change overnight, Gina, so don't expect me to. I'm a slob and I like being a slob. Dirt's never bothered me. But I'll try. I'll sincerely try, for your sake. What you said this morning made sense to me. It must get tiring for all the responsibility to rest on the woman's shoulders. Just don't expect a miracle, okay? Because miracles don't happen overnight."

Doubts crowded into Gina's consciousness, but she lifted her eyes and nodded hesitantly. "I guess all we can do is try."

"Yeah," he said frowning. "I guess."

She reached out tentatively and ran her hand down his cheek, feeling the beginnings of sexual quiverings deep in her midsection. "And about our priorities?"

"What about them?"

He stood unmoving, making it harder on her. She had to fight against her pride, but somehow she managed. "I think I'd like to give them a tryout."

"Oh?" He arched a brow and stood as still as a rock.

"Colin," she said. "Stop it, will you?"

"Stop what?"

"Stop making it hard on me!"

"Making what hard on you?"

She grabbed his hand and dragged him back to bed. "Colin Cassidy," she said, desire lowering her voice, "don't you *ever* play hard to get with me again. Is that clear? If I tell you to strip, you strip."

One corner of his mouth lifted lazily. "Is that a command I hear?"

"It sure is," she said, and unzipped the front of her sweatshirt.

Slowly, he unzipped his trousers. "If we're going to compromise, maybe you better let me issue a few commands, Longford."

She felt her heart swell with expectation. "Okay," she said softly.

"Why don't you take off the rest of those clothes and come to bed with me?" he suggested gently.

She didn't waste another instant arguing.

Twelve

The network's canceled a show already," Peter Davis announced exultantly two weeks later. "They want to air our first show next week. This is the break we've been waiting for!"

Gina flew into Colin's arms, hugging and kissing him. "I can't believe it," she said, her eyes glowing. "I thought we'd be lucky to get on in January, and here it is mid-November and they're already putting us on."

"Which means they could can us just as easily as they canned the other show," Colin said darkly, turning and walking away.

Startled by Colin's lack of enthusiasm, Gina glanced at Peter, who raised his eyebrows then turned away to talk with his assistant.

"Colin?" she said when she caught up to him at the coffee machine. "You okay?"

"Sure. Never better." He put some coins in the machine and then cursed and kicked the machine when it didn't produce the coffee.

Gina put a hand on his arm. "Hey," she said, laughing softly, "what's the matter? We just got the best news we could get and you're out here mauling a coffee machine. We should be celebrating. Let's stop and buy some champagne on the way home."

"If you want to celebrate, buy yourself some champagne. All I know is, I've never counted my chickens before they hatched and I don't intend to start now."

Gina stepped back, her face troubled. After living with Colin for two weeks, she was beginning to understand him even better. Any time there was a chance that he might succeed or fail, he became extraordinarily defensive and automatically assumed the latter. His attitude was particularly troubling, because from all she knew about him, he was the kind of marvelous man who had the ability to land on his feet and turn any failure into success. The only one who didn't believe in Colin Cassidy was Colin Cassidy, who was, ironically, the only one who really counted. She could stand on the sidelines and cheer him on for years, but until he believed in himself, he would never truly accept his successes.

"Beginning to share my doubts, Gina?" he asked, finally managing to produce a cup of coffee by rocking the coffee machine from side to side.

"No," she said angrily, "I'm not. Look at you." She indicated the machine. "You're the most persistent man I know. You run into a broken coffee machine and refuse to give in to it. By sheer dint of persistent effort, you *force* it to produce coffee for you, and yet you have the audacity to predict that you'll fail." She stepped closer, her eyes blazing with belief in him. "You couldn't fail if you tried, Cassidy. You're a natural winner. You have talent, looks and best of all, a wonderful brain. You know the movie business inside out. You have a great reviewing style, a natural camera presence, and you turn any woman's knees to jelly who's watching you. You're a guaranteed success, and the fact that I'm along is just extra icing on the cake, because *I* don't intend to fail, Cassidy.''

Her eyes sparked with anger and frustration, then she dug her forefinger into his chest and pushed against it, hard. ''So don't let me hear any more doomsday talk from you, okay? Because I'm not listening.'' She whirled on her heel, then paused and turned back. ''And we're buying champagne tonight and we're celebrating, because there's no way on earth we're going to bomb out. Is that clear, Cassidy?''

He lifted one corner of his mouth as he leaned against the wall and watched her. ''Yeah, it's pretty clear, Longford,'' he said softly.

She felt her stomach turn over, felt her heart begin to pound, felt an instant desire to hike up her skirt right there in the hall and let him have his way with her. ''We'll drink the champagne in bed, okay, Cassidy?'' she said sternly.

He sipped his coffee, watching her over the rim of his cup. Finally he nodded. ''Okay, Longford.''

Her face blossomed into a huge smile, then, turning, she bounded away, her steps filled with joy, her spirit racing with the wind. They were going to do it; she knew it in her bones. Somehow, in some way, she and Colin Cassidy were going to make it, in every way possible.

Gina frowned as she unwrapped the gold foil on the champagne bottle, then struggled with the wire that held the cork. ''Can you remove this cork?'' she asked Colin absently, still fiddling with the wires.

Colin looked up from reading *Variety*. ''I can, but I prefer not to,'' he said quietly.

Startled, Gina looked up at him and her frown deepened. "How come?"

"Because I told you once before today, I don't think we have anything to celebrate, so I don't want any blasted champagne."

Gina's spirits plummeted. That was all it took—just a few pessimistic words from Colin could change gold to drab, a sunny day to a cloudy one. How was she ever going to change him?

Her eyes widened and she looked away quickly. Didn't she know enough by now to realize that people only changed if and when they wanted to? She could stand on her head and play a tuba for the next twenty years in an effort to get Colin to change, but if he didn't want to, he wouldn't. It was as simple as that.

She raised her eyes and surreptitiously watched him as he read the paper, feeling her heart swell inside her, knowing that she was past falling in love with him—she was already *in* love with him. She felt her heart turn over at his lack of self-confidence, yet she knew he had to learn to believe in himself on his own. She could lecture him for years, yell at him for hours, and he would remain the same. She supposed all she could do was love him just the way he was. It was the only gift she could give him—her love and her undying belief in him.

"Well," she said, shrugging philosophically, "if you won't share the champagne with me, will you at least open the damned bottle?"

Colin looked up from the newspaper, then slowly set it down and stretched out his long legs, watching her thoughtfully. "You're a stubborn lass, aren't you?"

She nodded vivaciously. "Very stubborn. And I bought this bottle of imported bubbly, so I'm gonna drink it. In bed. Stark naked." She got up from the couch and flounced toward the bedroom. "And if *you're* so stubborn that you won't join me, then it's your loss, Cassidy, not mine."

"I thought you couldn't get the cork out," he yelled after her.

"I'll break the damn top off," she yelled back, waving the bottle over her head. "You know, like they do when they christen ships." She pantomimed holding the bottle by the end and slamming it against something, then waved jauntily and blew Colin a kiss before disappearing into the bedroom and closing the door decisively behind her.

A moment later, Colin was in the bathroom, taking the bottle she held poised over the sink from her hands. "You weren't actually going to crack the top off the bottle on the sink, were you?" he asked incredulously.

"Sure," she said. "Why not?"

"The sink's porcelain, Gina," he explained patiently, wrapping a towel around the bottle and beginning to twist the cork out gently. "You'd end up breaking the sink along with the bottle."

"Oh."

He glanced up at her, his dark eyes gleaming with amusement. "'Oh,' she says. As if it never occurred to her that she was about to precipitate a major plumbing emergency."

She perched on the toilet and brought her knees up, wrapping her arms around her legs and resting her chin atop her knees. "Yeah, but I'll bet you could fix it," she said, eyeing him hungrily. Right now, the champagne wasn't nearly as appealing as he was.

"I could turn off the water supply, but even *I* couldn't fix a cracked porcelain sink, Gina," he said, popping out the cork and watching as a puff of bluish vapor emerged from the chilled bottle. He draped the towel over his arm and turned to her, bowing formally. "Your glass, madam?"

She grinned as she reached for the glass on the edge of the sink. "Pour, Jeeves," she said, putting on a rich, upper-class British accent, "then turn down the sheets in the bedroom, will you?" She gave him a seductive look and sidled up to him, tracing a finger down his brawny arm. "My husband's away, you know, Jeeves, and I . . . er . . . I've always found you rather attractive. . . ."

He grinned at her, shaking his head. "You have a vivid fantasy life, don't you, Gina?"

She sipped the champagne, then wrinkled her nose in pleasure. She drank again greedily, draining the glass, then held it out for more. He refilled it and she tugged him by the arm into the bedroom. "Now then," she said, looking into his eyes as she sipped the champagne, "undress me."

"Perhaps you'd better put the glass down first," he suggested softly. "Otherwise, it might spill."

"But isn't that the point of champagne in the bedroom?" she asked innocently. "Spilling it and then licking it up?"

"Gina," Colin said huskily, taking the glass from her and putting it down, then taking her in his arms. "Don't tempt me."

"But I *want* to tempt you," she said huskily. She ran her hands down his muscular arms and drew in a deep, languorous breath. "Do you know, Colin Cassidy, that you have the most extraordinary body? Every time I look at you, I get these strange little impulses to seduce you." She put her hand behind his neck and drew his head down to hers, dropping a moist kiss on his mouth as she slid her fingers into the opening of his shirt and rubbed his chest. "It doesn't matter where we are," she continued throatily, beginning to unbutton his shirt as she dropped soft, seductive kisses on his face and neck. "Matter of fact, I get these impulses at the most inconvenient times, like when we're taping and you're being particularly obstinate about a movie, or when we're driving home and we're stopped at a red light, and there are other cars around. That's the hardest, because it's all I can do to keep my hands off you."

As if to illustrate what she meant, she unzipped his trousers and reached inside, obviously pleased by his arousal. "Like this," she whispered softly.

"Gina," he groaned, pulling her closer, his arms hard around her. "You drive me crazy, you know that, woman?"

She finished unbuttoning his shirt then slid it from his shoulders. He let it drop to the floor, then picked her up and strode quickly to the bed, his breathing husky.

She put her arms around his neck and pulled his head down to hers and whispered throatily against his lips, "I want you, Colin Cassidy—lying down, sitting up or standing, any way you want me, I want you. Is that clear?"

"Extraordinarily," he said, pulling her blouse from her waistband and easing his hand under it to caress her lace-covered skin.

She sucked in her breath on a gasp of ecstasy, then sighed longingly as he unhooked her bra and covered her aching breast with his hot, seeking mouth. She ran her hands into his hair and held his head to her breast, her eyes closed as she savored the rapture of his tongue and lips on her nipple. Slowly, gently, he aroused it, until it was as hard and round as a pebble in his mouth and she was writhing on the bed beneath him, moaning incoherently for more.

He transferred his attention to her other breast, and she ran her hands down his smooth, broad back, then thrust them beneath his trousers and kneaded his buttocks. "Colin," she said breathlessly, "hurry, darling."

"Hurry?" he asked softly, raising up on an elbow to look down into her desire-drugged eyes. He lifted one corner of his lips in a lazy grin then began to undress her. "I don't think we want to hurry this, Gina," he said, dropping kisses on her breasts, then burning a fiery trail downward to her abdomen. "I don't think we want to hurry this at all."

His tongue darted into her navel and she gasped with pleasure. "I think we do," she said, her voice even more breathless. Perhaps it was the effect of the champagne, but for some reason, her senses seemed more heightened tonight, so that everything Colin did seemed larger than life. His touch was filled with magic, his hands and lips and tongue were potent instruments designed to bring her the ultimate in fulfillment. She lay back, her hips swaying back and forth. "Hurry," she whispered. "Hurry, I can't wait."

"Ah," he said, running his tongue down her abdomen, "then perhaps I should do something to make you feel better, hmm?" He parted her legs and lowered his head, inching his tongue along her hipbone and continuing down. She gave an incredible gasp of pleasure and felt radiant rockets go off deep inside her. "Oh, yes," she moaned, holding his head to her and arching her back. "Oh, yes."

"You don't want me to hurry now, do you?" he whispered.

She shook her head, her eyes closed, her mouth opened softly as small cries of pleasure escaped. "No," she finally whispered. "Please, darling, don't hurry. Don't—" she took a deep breath as his tongue lazily traced her contours, then let it out "—hurry."

"I won't," he said, rising up and reaching for the champagne. "In fact, I think I'll have some champagne."

She felt her immediate sexual need dissipate and began to smile. "You will?" she said, pleasure at his decision filling her with warmth. "Oh, Colin, I'm so happy you'll share the champagne with me."

He filled her glass then looked around. "But we have a problem, my dear," he said softly. "No glass for me."

"I'll get you—" she said, only to have him lay his finger across her lips to silence her.

"No, there's a better way."

She lay back, thinking he'd drink directly from the bottle, but to her complete surprise and shock, he poured some onto her stomach. It pooled in her navel, but a few drops escaped and trickled between her thighs. She felt the shock of the fizzing liquid, then the even greater shock of his tongue, licking it from her gently, lovingly, following the path it made until she felt herself rising as if on a magic carpet, racing into the night wind, leaving the earth and all she'd ever known behind.

With Colin, from that moment, she went where she'd never been, into a sensual land where pleasure reigned supreme, where his slightest touch aroused such joy that she felt herself melt and cry out in rapture. Dizzy, dancing on clouds of enchantment, she gave herself to him fully, loving him as she'd never loved any man. She trusted him so completely that sometime in the night, when she knew that there would never be another man for her as long as she lived, she cried out his name and fell asleep, whispering, "I love you...."

The following Saturday night, Gina invited Peter Davis and the taping crew to her house to watch their first show air on television. Gina hurried to and fro, nervous as a cat, freshening drinks, emptying ashtrays, doling out pizza, then pausing to gnaw on her thumbnail and glance at Colin, who seemed completely impervious to nerves.

"How do you *do* it?" she whispered loudly when they were both alone in the kitchen just before the show was to come on. "I'm sick. I feel as if I'm at sea and there are thirty-foot waves crashing around me, and here you are, as cool as the proverbial cucumber."

Colin took her in his arms and placed her hand against his heart. "It doesn't show outwardly, but perhaps this will tell you something of what I feel."

His heart was pounding furiously under her hand, and she felt her own nerves disappear in the desire to soothe his. She rested her head against his chest and stroked him lovingly, realizing that his simple gesture of revealing his fear to her meant more than almost anything he could have done. By showing her his fear in such a way, he was also showing he trusted her. She held him tightly, tears misting her eyes, then she looked up at him. "What do they say on stage when they want to wish someone luck?" she asked softly. "Break a leg?"

He smiled down at her and hugged her tightly. "Well, we've already read the television previews, and no one thought we were even important enough to get more than a mention. Anyway, we're not the kind of show that everyone's going to watch, and it *is* Saturday night, just after the news, after all, so lots of people will be getting ready to go out. We'll be lucky if we come in last on the Nielsen ratings." He shrugged. "I guess there's nothing to be nervous about."

She shook her head at him as she straightened his collar, her eyes dancing. "You always manage to find a way to rationalize, don't you, Cassidy?" she asked, laughing softly. "It's Saturday night, so we won't do well. Or it's just after the news, so we won't do well, or it's not the kind of show many people watch." She hugged him tightly and rested her head against his chest. "Just remember one thing, Cassidy, I believe in us, okay? We're gonna be a smash."

"I'm not so sure," he said, pushing her away and preparing to return to the living room.

Gina stepped back quietly, allowing him the space he needed, yet feeling his rejection as a cruel blow. She wished he could turn to her in his need, but she knew that that would only come in time, if at all. Love was a slow game of chance. Sometimes it took root and flourished; other times it died almost as quickly as it had seemed to spring to life. But she knew there was only one kind of love that mattered, the deep, committed kind, the kind of love that stayed beside the loved one and didn't give up when the going got rough, the kind that fought for a foothold, that believed when there seemed to be no reason to believe.

She would wait then, and she wouldn't give up. She loved Colin Cassidy with all the fierce passion of which she was capable. And she realized something she'd never known about herself before—that she believed in the power of love, believed in its magic ability to turn the grumpiest man into a smiling charmer, to grant confidence to the most fearful. Silently she offered a small prayer for this complicated man she loved so much, for this man who had known such pain, yet who refused to discuss it, who hid it behind a curmudgeon's outlook and a refusal to get truly involved.

"Oh, please," she whispered softly, tears misting her eyes, "I don't give a fig about myself. Make it a success for him. Somehow, let him see what he is, let him walk out of the darkness and into the sunshine. And if for some reason it doesn't succeed, help him to know it wasn't his fault. Help him see that I love him no matter what he does, if he fails or succeeds."

She dabbed at her eyes and straightened her shoulders and walked into the living room, her eyes suddenly dancing with excitement and laughter, because she knew it would be easier on him if she pretended to be happy rather than nervous. It was strange, she thought, taking a seat next to him and surreptitiously putting her hand in his, how easy life was when you were motivated by love for another. Though she cared about her own success, she felt a selfless interest in Colin's.

Bemused, she sat and watched their logo appear on the screen, then she realized it—they were truly a team. Sometime during the past few weeks, she'd stopped working alone and fallen into step beside Colin Cassidy.

Thirteen

Peter stared down at the negative review of *Hollywood Report Card*, then threw the newspaper across the room. "So what does he know?" he growled, then yelled, "On the set! Gina! Colin! Let's get cracking, we've got a TV program to produce here."

Colin sat slouched in his chair, sipping coffee, looking as unconcerned at the review as if it weren't his show being panned. Gina watched Colin nervously then walked quickly onto the set and took her place next to him.

"I suppose you're going to say 'I told you so,'" she said lightly.

"Nope," Colin said easily. "I never say that, even when it's true."

Gina sighed. "Look, it's only one review, Colin. Plenty of TV shows have been panned by the critics only to go on and be very successful. Anyway, like I said, he's only one critic. The others haven't written anything yet."

"Give 'em time," Colin said dryly.

"Well," Gina said, shrugging lightly, "one thing can be said for you—you're taking it well. I haven't seen you in this good a mood since I met you."

"I'm always in a good mood when I'm proved right," Colin said, smiling lazily.

Gina looked at him thoughtfully, then shook her head. "But you're not right yet, Colin. Our first show wasn't our best. This Saturday, our second will be on, and it was ten-times better than our first, and the week after that, we really hit our stride, so don't count those chickens you're always talking about. You just may have a hit on your hands before you know it."

"You really *are* an optimist, aren't you?" Colin asked, chuckling.

"Yes, I am," Gina said stoutly, anger at him beginning to sizzle in her veins. "And I hope someday it rubs off on you, because you could use it!" With that, she turned toward the cameras and began to go over her notes.

"You mad at me, Gina?" Colin asked quietly.

She hesitated, then looked up from her notes. "No, I'm not mad, I'm just tired of your attitude. When is it going to hit you, Colin Cassidy, that *you* are responsible for what you do with your life. You can sit back and predict failure and let it come, or you can get up and fight for the success that you deserve and reap the rewards. It's up to you, Colin, yet for some reason, you won't see it that way. You seem to think you're a failure with a big red F written across your forehead. Well, you know who wrote that F, Colin? You did."

By now, she was so angry she was trembling, but just then Peter called for quiet on the set and she had to compose her features. When the lights went up, she was smiling easily, ready to give a glowing review to a new comedy.

"You did that well," Colin said when they'd finished taping for the day.

"Did what well?" she asked, fiddling with her mike.

"Went from lecturing me to giving the best damned review I've ever heard you do."

Her head came up and she stared at Colin, then slowly detached her mike, hidden beneath the lapel of her suit jacket. "Was I lecturing you?" she asked quietly. "Is that how it seemed?"

"Yup. Ms. Longford, the eternal optimist, telling her recalcitrant partner that he should take his head out of the sand and smell the daisies. Think positively. Grin and sit back and watch success just come rolling in."

Quietly Gina looked down at the notes she'd crumpled in her hand. "I guess it *did* sound a bit like the old 'pull yourself up by the bootstraps' lecture, didn't it?" she asked softly.

Colin sighed. "Uh-huh. I've heard it a million times, from a million different women, and it's never worked once, Gina, so why don't you just give up and admit defeat?"

She lifted her eyes and looked at Colin, then shrugged and rose from the chair. "Okay," she said. "It's your life, Colin. Live it the way you want."

With that, she walked out of the studio. A few minutes later, Colin joined her in the car. She waited for him to close the door and fasten his seat belt, then she drove off at a sedate pace, her face composed, her mind at peace.

"You really *are* angry at me, aren't you?" Colin finally asked.

She turned warm eyes to his. "No, sweetheart, I'm not angry," she said softly.

He frowned, as if he couldn't quite understand her mood. "Well, why did you stop arguing and walk off like that if you're not angry?"

"Because I realized you were right. If you've really heard the same lecture from a million different women and it's never worked, why should I expect to make it work? You are what you are, Colin, and I guess I just realized that's good enough for me."

Now his frown deepened. "What do you mean, that's good enough for you?"

She glanced at him, smiling. "Just what it sounds like. I think it'd be great if you were the most confident man in the world, because from my perspective, you deserve to be, but if you're filled with doubts about yourself, I guess there's nothing I can say to take them away. You'll have to deal with them in your own way on your own terms. I can give you all the pep talks in the world, but until you're ready to believe what I say, they won't work." She downshifted and pulled into her driveway. "So, that's it, Colin. No more pep talks. No more lectures." She pulled the car to a stop and turned to face him. "There's only one more thing I want to say—"

"I knew it," Colin said darkly. "I knew you couldn't drop it. No woman has ever been able to."

Anger flared through Gina, but she bit it back. "I just wanted to say this, Colin," she said quietly, gathering her pocketbook and opening the car door. "I love you, just the way you are. In my book, you'll always be the greatest, and if you never change, that'll be all right with me."

With that, she closed the car door softly and strode briskly toward her cottage. She was shaking inside, but she knew she'd said what she had to say. It wasn't easy telling him how much she cared, because admitting she cared left her vulnerable, and being vulnerable to more pain in her life was the last thing she wanted. To salvage her pride, she could have kept quiet, but she realized there was something at stake a lot more important than her pride, and that was her love for Colin. Even if he didn't return her love, even if the past few weeks of living together had meant only convenient, casual sex to him, they'd meant everything to her, and she wasn't going to take the easy way out and deny her feelings.

She walked into the house and saw that Colin had left three or four old newspapers scattered around the floor. There were two empty beer bottles on a table and half a bag of peanuts, their shells littering the floor around his favorite chair. Ordinarily she would rush over and begin cleaning up, all the while muttering low curses at the way men lived like pigs, but today she merely hung up her coat and went to her bedroom.

For some reason, the mess in the living room didn't seem to matter very much. It was almost homey, to walk into her usually immaculate home and see Colin's litter scattered about. She realized that she'd spent the duration of her first marriage using all her energy to change her husband, when she should have been using it to change herself. She couldn't change Jack, just as she couldn't change Colin. There was only one person in the world she could change—herself. From now on, she would work on it, though she had no illusions that it would be easy.

She surmised it meant giving up the feeling of control, and for Gina that was especially difficult. It was far easier to get her own way and have the other person do the changing, than to change her own ways or learn to compromise. She leaned forward and looked at herself in the mirror. "Keep thy own house in order," she said out loud. "Forget about everyone else's."

Then the bedroom door opened and Colin appeared. "Why the hell did you walk away from me?" he asked roughly.

She turned slowly. "Because I thought what I said might take you by surprise and you'd need a little time to think."

"Oh." He looked baffled, then ran his hand through his hair and cleared his throat. "Look, Gina..."

"Yes?"

He frowned and sighed and looked as if he wanted to be anywhere but here. "Look, I don't want to hurt you, Gina."

She felt her heart constrict, felt the first feeling of foreboding, but she held it back, urged it into the darkness, didn't want to face what she feared might be coming. She took a deep breath and forced herself to speak calmly. "That's kind of you, Colin," she said quietly.

He groaned and sat down on the bed. "Look, Gina, women are always falling for me, and I'm not the best bet, you know what I mean?"

"No, I'm afraid I don't."

He groaned again and said, "At least make this easy on me, Gina."

"Why?" she asked. "I've got a feeling it's not going to be easy on me. Why should I make it easy on you?"

"Gina, I don't want to hurt you."

"You said that."

"Gina," he pleaded.

She turned away, knotting her hands into fists to hold back the angry words she wanted to fling at him. Damn, she was sick of his attitude! She would like to kick some sense into him, but she knew it wouldn't do any good. She had to trust that the past few weeks together had begun to set the pattern for what she hoped would become a lifetime together.

"Look, Gina, maybe I should move out."

She turned around then, her face calm, her manner in control. "Why? What's changed?"

"Gina, everything's changed. All a woman has to do is mention the word love and everything changes automatically. It's all different now."

"Yes," she said dryly, "it's getting serious. You've got more to lose now, don't you, Colin? Before, it was just playacting. As long as I didn't talk about love or feelings, you felt safe, but I said the dirty L word, didn't I? I upped the ante. So now you're going to run and hide, is that it? Is that how you play the game, Colin? Every time there's a chance that you could get *really* involved, do you duck out?"

His dark eyes flickered with anger, then he turned and walked away. "I'll sleep in the guest room tonight."

"Coward," she taunted softly.

He turned to look back at her, a muscle in his jaw working restlessly. "What did you say?"

"I called you a coward," she said quietly. "What's the matter? Don't you like that?"

He closed the door and walked slowly back toward her. "No, not particularly."

"Good," she said cheerfully. "That means there's hope for you."

He shook his head, as if to clear out cobwebs. "I don't know what the hell's going on between us, Gina, but I'm not sure I like it."

"Colin, honey," she said, taking him by the hand and leading him toward the bed. "What's happening between us is we're falling in love. We're getting involved. It's uncomfortable for lots of people, especially men, because it means exposing feelings, and being vulnerable, and facing the possibility of rejection and pain." She reached out and began to unbutton his shirt. "But I'm afraid there's no other way for it to happen. You have to take the bad with the good. Oh, by the way, did I tell you your critique of Winston's new film was great? I never thought about it in those terms until I was sitting there this afternoon listening to you."

Colin lay back, staring up at Gina as if he'd never seen her before. Finally he said, "Is that why you had that admiring glint in your eyes?"

Laughing softly, she bent to kiss him tenderly. "Partly," she murmured, reaching inside his shirt and running her fingertips down his brawny chest. "Though there was another reason."

"And what was that?" he asked, his voice deepening as it always did when he wanted to make love to her.

"Ohh," she said, sighing wistfully and lying down beside him. "I just got to thinking about the way you drink champagne...."

Chuckling, he went up on his elbow and looked down at her. "Is that a hint?"

"If we have any champagne, I wouldn't mind opening a bottle," she said innocently.

"I'm afraid we don't have any, honey," he said, leaning over to unbutton her blouse.

"Then let's pretend," she whispered.

A slow smile broke over his face and he gathered her into his strong arms. "Great idea," he murmured softly. "Why don't we?"

"No news is good news," Peter said curtly a week later. "The network executives are playing their cards close to their chests. They're not saying what they think about *Hollywood Report Card*." He sighed mightily and whacked the script against his leg. "But this is our fourth week on the air, so let's get cracking, people, we've got taping to do!"

Gina and Colin took their places and fell into the routine that was becoming more and more comfortable for them. Halfway through the taping, Colin made a mistake but covered it up so well with an ad lib that they left it in. Afterward everyone stood around the monitor watching the tape, laughing at the natural way Colin covered his goof. Another camera angle had caught Gina reacting with a look of delight on her face and a string of giggles, so they spliced that in, adding to the spontaneity of the show.

"Who knows?" Peter said, grinning. "Maybe we'll win 'em over by *not* being the polished professionals we've tried to be!"

Two weeks before Christmas, Gina suggested they buy a Christmas tree. Colin laughed and gestured out the window. "*Buy* a tree? When you've got half a forest right outdoors? Let's just take a walk and cut one."

They put on their parkas and wandered hand in hand through the woods until they found the perfect tree, then as they dragged it home behind them, it began to snow.

"Oh, Colin," Gina said, lifting her rapt face to the chilled flakes that drifted from the slate-gray sky. "Oh, it's perfect."

He put his arms around her and drew her closer. "Yes," he said softly. "It is."

She looked up at him and smiled into his eyes, feeling as warm as if she were on a Caribbean island. Things were beginning to change, little by little. She'd noticed that since she'd stopped cleaning up after Colin, the messes stayed where he'd left them for days—until finally he realized she wasn't going to clean up for him and he ended up cleaning up after himself, without her ever having said a word.

She didn't whine, she didn't meddle, she didn't demand. She merely went about her own life, cleaning up after herself as she always had and letting Colin live the way he wanted to. Slowly she'd begun to see him taking responsibility for his own messes. He stacked the papers now instead of scattering them around his chair. He put away his beer bottles, picked up the peanut shells, cleaned the tub without arguing.

Sometimes, she caught him looking at her quizzically, as if he were trying to figure out what she was doing, but wasn't quite able to put his finger on the changes in their lives or how they'd come about. They lived as if in a dream, enchanted with each other, sharing their concerns, opening up, talking, laughing, making love in her bed, which had now become theirs.

And then one day early in January, they found out their show was a smash hit.

"They love it, I tell ya!" Peter said, pacing back and forth excitedly in his office. Gina and Colin were seated before his desk, staring at him, both looking a little dumbfounded. Peter smacked the papers he was holding. "It's all right here, in the rating sheets. Focus interviews. Polls—they all say the same thing—*Hollywood Report Card* is a smash."

He turned to Gina and Colin, his eyes gleaming. "When your contracts are up, you'll get raises you won't believe. You'll be rolling in dough. The network bigwigs want to move you to a new time, but I talked them out of it. I told 'em if it's working, don't fix it, and thank God, they listened." He sat on the edge of the couch in his office and beamed. "I tell you, guys, this is the most wonderful news of my life. Of yours too, I'll bet. *People* wants to do a cover story on you, and *TV Guide* wants to do a feature, and *West 57th* is interested, too." Peter grinned from ear to ear. "Ain't life great?"

Gina laughed uncertainly, then shook her head. "Well, yeah, I guess so. It's just a little hard to take in. One minute you're a syndicated newspaper columnist in Hartford, Connecticut, and the next you're cohost of a smash TV show, on the covers of magazines." She glanced at Colin. "What do you think? Can you handle it?"

Colin slid lower in his chair, frowning. "Success? I don't know. I've had too much experience with failure."

"Ah, nonsense," Peter said, grinning enthusiastically. "You'll handle it okay when the show gets nominated for an Emmy."

"An Emmy?" Colin echoed incredulously.

"Ah, only some kind of technical thing probably. You know, best editing or production or something, but hey, it's nice to be associated with a winner for a change, eh, Colin?"

Colin smiled uncertainly and Gina felt those strange feelings of foreboding she hadn't felt in over a month. "Come on," she said, taking Colin's hand. "Let's buy some champagne and celebrate. You told me you never counted your chickens till they hatched. Well, honey, they've come home to roost, and it looks like we're gonna need two bottles of champagne."

Restlessly Colin walked back and forth, gnawing on the inside of his mouth. "Are you sure about those ratings, Peter?"

"Does a TV studio need lights? Of course, I'm sure. Here, take a look yourself."

Colin scanned the piles of statistics then handed them to Gina and resumed his pacing. Meanwhile, Peter stared at him, puzzled.

"What's the matter with you, Colin? You should be dancing in the aisles of every movie theater in the state. You're going to be famous, pal. *Famous!* Today, in the movie section of the paper, I saw a quote from you guys in an ad: 'A grade of A+ for *Guardians of the Sky*—Gina Longford and Colin Cassidy, *Hollywood Report Card.*'"

Peter shook his head admiringly. "I tell ya, you've made it. *We've* made it! It's terrific, huh?"

"Yeah, Pete," Colin said absently, "it's terrific."

Gina turned away, her heart hammering nervously. She should be ecstatic, on top of the world, celebrating. Instead, she felt more apprehensive than she ever had in all her time with Colin. Perhaps he'd said more than he realized when he'd said he didn't know if he could handle success, since he had so much experience with failure.

Gina felt her heart dip painfully. Perhaps Colin's problem wasn't really fear of being a failure. Perhaps all along, he'd really been afraid of success....

Fourteen

That night, Gina and Colin sat in front of the fireplace, sharing a bottle of champagne. It had begun to snow, and the white flakes drifted like clouds in the dark night air. Gina was filled with a confusion of emotions as she watched Colin—love and warmth, sadness and fear, pain and anxiety. He was so quiet he'd barely responded to any of her happy chatter, and now they both sat in silence, Colin staring into the flames, Gina watching him.

"Talk to me, Colin," she urged softly, pulling him back against her and putting her arms around him. "What are you thinking right now? Don't close me out, honey."

He took her hand and kissed her palm, then squeezed her hand and turned to face her. "I was remembering, Gina."

"Remembering?"

"My mother, when I was a kid, and how I felt when she left us. I can remember how she used to get so tired of doing housework and she'd yell at me for leaving my toys around, and—'' He broke off, frowning hard. "I remember when Dad told me she'd left, I went into my bedroom and saw that I'd left out all my toys again, and I thought to myself, 'She left because of me. She left because I made her work so hard and she couldn't take it anymore.'"

"Oh, Colin," Gina said, hugging him tightly, closing her eyes against the tears that threatened to overwhelm her. "Oh, sweetheart." Guilt at her own ranting and raving overwhelmed her, and she sat back, her eyes mirroring her pain. "I'm sorry, Colin," she whispered softly. "You must feel at times as if every woman on earth is finding fault with you."

"I *did*," he said slowly, thoughtfully. "When I met you that first day, I told you I thought I was a genuine misogynist, that I really hated women. But I'm changing. I've been sitting here, looking back at the past, seeing my mother through eyes that you opened. When you told me how frustrating housework can be, I began to understand what it must have been like for my mother, a twenty-year-old girl with dreams of being a star. All my life, I've blamed myself for her leaving, thinking she didn't love me and that it was somehow *my* fault, but I've begun to see that maybe the problem was with her. Maybe she just wasn't cut out for being a mother and a housewife. Maybe it wasn't that I wasn't lovable, but that she just couldn't love me in the way I needed to be loved."

Gina nodded quietly, hugging him tightly, her love for him filling her, so that she hurt so much for him she wanted to cry. She couldn't stand the thought of the pain he'd carried around all these years. She wanted to somehow take it from him, leaving him filled with love and warmth and happiness. She wanted only good things for Colin but realized that life wasn't always good, that people weren't always wise and kind, that endings weren't always happy. "I'd

say that's a pretty good analysis," she said softly. "I'm glad
you've realized that she didn't leave because of you."

She rubbed her face against his arm lovingly. "I hope
you've begun to realize that I love you, no matter how messy
you are. When I yelled at you in the beginning, Colin, it
wasn't *your* problem, it was *mine*. I wasn't mature enough
to let you be yourself. I had to try to change you. In my hu-
bris, I thought I was the only one who knew how life should
work—that everyone should be neat and clean and orderly.
It never hit me until later, when I'd fallen hopelessly in love
with you and realized that I loved you no matter *how* messy
you were, that no one has the 'right' answers, because there
aren't any. What's right for me may be terribly wrong for
you. I had to learn to live and let live. I had to learn to stop
trying to control you and just let you be yourself."

"Oh, Gina," he said, taking her in his arms and hugging
her tightly, swaying with her back and forth, cradling her,
his face filled with wonder.

"It's going to be all right now, Colin," Gina said, smiling at him confidently. "Everything's going to be fine between us."

He let go of her and turned away, his face suddenly
clouded with fear. "Don't say that, Gina. Just don't say
that. All my life, things have ended up rotten. I'd begin to
think I'd found a woman to love and she'd end up leaving
or I'd get tired of her and leave, or a job wouldn't work
out...." He stared into the fireplace, clearly troubled. "The
thing is, Gina, you're just too innocent, too trusting. You
see silver linings in every cloud. When *I* see clouds, I expect
rain and duck for cover."

"I think I see what you mean. You're so used to having
problems happen, that you begin to expect them."

"No," he said, "not exactly. What I mean is, I never take
success or happiness for granted. I always look ahead, trying

to sniff out a potential problem, because I know life's like that—just when you think everything's going fine, wham! Along comes a locomotive and it rams right into you.''

She nodded thoughtfully, realizing that he was the balance she needed so badly in her life. Emotional and headstrong, she'd rolled through life like a cannonball loose on board a ship, a reckless woman who'd let her emotions rule, to the possible danger of herself and everyone around her.

She felt her throat close up at the thought of how much she needed Colin, at the possibility that he didn't need her as much. What if he got tired of her? What if he suddenly wanted to move on? She would be devastated. She didn't think she could live without him, didn't know if she'd want to even try.

''Gina?''

She looked up quickly, relieved that he couldn't read her mind. ''Yes?''

He put his thumb under her chin and raised her face to his, tilting his head as he studied her expression. ''What are *you* thinking? You're really good at getting me to talk and open up, but sometimes you don't always do the same.''

She nodded, smiling ruefully as she wrapped her arms around her legs and rested her chin on her knees. She stared into the fireplace, wondering if she could ever tell Colin what she was feeling. She wasn't good at being vulnerable. Like Colin had said, she was great at getting *others* to admit vulnerability and need, but she reserved a special clause in the contract for herself. She was the kind of person, she realized with a sinking heart, who said *Do as I say, not as I do.*

She heaved an apprehensive sigh and delved into it: ''I was thinking how much I need you, how good you are for me. If I always see silver linings in the clouds, that's good to a point. But sometimes there isn't a silver lining there, and that's where your attitude comes in—it gives me balance. Without you, I'd be unrealistically optimistic.''

"And without you," he said softly, "I'd be unrealistically pessimistic."

She raised her head and stared at him, her eyes filled with a mixture of hope and fear. "What do you mean?"

"I guess I mean we're a good team, Gina. We work well together."

She felt her heart plummet, felt all her hopes dash to the ground. Here he was, talking about how well they worked together, when she only cared about how they felt about each other. Their silly television program was the last thing on her mind right now, and the only thing on his. "Oh," she said, disappointment flooding her. "Yeah, I guess we are at that." She shrugged cheerfully, deciding to pretend and just make the best of it. "The show's a success, so I can't argue with you there."

"Now *that's* a problem," he said.

"What is?" she asked, puzzled.

"That you can't argue with me. I've kinda gotten to like our arguments. They spice up my life. Most women never give me a hard time. You do. I like that."

She stared, nonplussed. "You do?"

"Yup, I do."

Her hopes began to rise, cautiously. "Well, uh, are we talking *Hollywood Report Card*-type arguments, or... um...domestic ones?"

"Well, maybe we should talk about the show first," he said slowly.

"I see," she said slowly. "Well, what about it?"

"Statistics rarely lie, Gina, and those that Pete showed us today were reliable ones, so I guess we *do* have a hit on our hands. I'm just wondering how we're going to handle it."

She shrugged. "Just keep doing what we're doing, I suppose. What else can we do?"

"Well, what about the fame part? Don't you want your picture on the cover of *People* magazine?"

"I can't say that's been one of my goals in life," she said ironically. "I'm glad the show's a hit. I love the movies, Colin, just as much as you do. Reviewing is my job, and the show's success can only mean good things for my career, but the fame part?" She frowned uneasily. "I'm not so sure I like that part of it. Maybe I'll have to get used to it, but for my part, I'd like to take it easy. Go into it slowly, not go overboard. I've seen a lot of talented people get caught up in the glamour and glitz of success and lose sight of what's really important—their work. I guess I just want to keep doing what we've been doing and let the fame take care of itself. If we *have* to do a little publicity, okay, but I'd rather spend my spare time doing other things."

"Such as?"

"Well, pretty much doing what we're—what I'm doing now." She corrected herself hastily and picked up the fireplace poker and gave the logs a hearty jab.

"What you're doing now?" Colin asked, suddenly shifting uncomfortably.

Gina glanced at him quickly, then looked away. God, this communicating stuff was awkward! He was rubbing his jaw, looking distracted, and she wondered if that meant he was going to suggest that he move out. Suppressing a groan, she lay back on the rug, staring up at the ceiling, wondering why people thought war was crazy when communication between just two people was so ridiculously difficult. If two people couldn't even understand each other, how were millions of people supposed to succeed?

"You don't look happy, Gina," Colin said quietly.

"I'm not," she said mournfully, still staring disconsolately at the ceiling.

Colin sighed. "Well, maybe I'd better leave you alone for a while."

She swallowed painfully and stared at him, wide-eyed. "Why?"

"Well, maybe I'm the one who's making you unhappy."

"No!" she said urgently, sitting up and taking his hand. "No, *you're* not making me unhappy!"

"Well if I'm not, what is?"

She swallowed again, feeling as if a tree stump were lodged in her throat. "I'm afraid, Colin," she whispered finally, hanging on to his hand for dear life.

"Afraid? Gina Longford afraid?" Colin screwed up his eyes and gazed at her speculatively. "I'd never believe that in a million years if I hadn't heard it from your own mouth."

"Oh, I'm afraid, all right," she said, nodding energetically, her hair bouncing in response. "Oh, *boy*, am I afraid! I just cover it up real well. That's what all the loud explosions are—camouflage. I've always figured the louder I was, the less people would see through to the real me, the fearful me. Good ol' bombast, it works every time."

"So what are you afraid of right now?" Colin asked softly, his eyes curiously gentle.

She looked down at his hand in hers, examined the strong fingers, the callused palm, then squeezed it to her breasts. "I'm afraid of losing you," she whispered shakily. "I'm afraid you're going to get tired of me and move out. I'm afraid—"

"Go on," he urged gently.

"Oh!" She hit her forehead with her hand and rolled her eyes. "Oh, God, where to begin? You want fears, I'll give you fears. Let's see, I'm afraid you're going to run out on me because of that damned pessimistic attitude of yours. I'm afraid you won't even give us a chance, because *you're* afraid and you won't admit it. I'm afraid because I've already told you I love you and you've never said it, not even once. That's what *really* scares me," she said, her voice shaking even harder. "When a woman goes out on a limb and admits she loves someone, and he doesn't tell her he loves her back, boy, does she get scared." She rested her forehead in her hand and groaned out loud, and it all came tumbling out in one long jumbled-up stream of angst. "Oh, Colin, I'm scared to death you're going to leave and I can't live without you, I really can't. The thing of it is, I don't *want* to live without you. I *hate* neat now. I like your clutter. Whenever I walk in the house now and see your junk all over the place, I feel so good inside, because I know I've *got* someone, you know what I mean? I'm not alone. Oh, Colin," she moaned, unable to stem the flow of words now that the dam had burst, "I hate living alone. I *hate* it! Do you know the saddest sight on earth? I heard someone say it once—one lone toothbrush in the bathroom. And I agree. And, and...TV dinners for one. And shopping for one and cooking for one, and sitting in front of the fireplace alone, and...I don't know, I could go on for hours. But it's not that I like you here simply because you're company. If it was a roommate I wanted, I could advertise for one. It's *you*, Colin." She turned wide, fearful eyes to his. "It's you," she ended lamely, softly, more frightened than she'd ever been in her life.

"So I guess that brings us to the domestic part of our discussion, right?"

She stared at him, amazed that he could be so calm when she'd just spouted out all her fears in such a frenzy. "Yes," she said, feeling slightly out of sorts, "I guess it does."

One corner of his mouth quirked in amusement. "You're getting angry with me."

"A little," she agreed huffily.

"Why?"

"Why?" She stared at him in true amazement. "Because I just poured out my *heart* and you're sitting there as if I were reciting the damned Dow Jones average!"

He chuckled softly, then tried to stop, but it refused to be stopped. Slowly the chuckle escalated into outright laughter, a belly laugh if the truth be told. All the while, Gina sat and stared at him, wrath dancing in her green eyes.

"You insensitive cad," she said softly, menacingly. "You're *laughing* at me!"

"No," he said, his laughter slowly dying out, "no, honey, I'm not laughing at you. Not the way you mean, anyway." He gathered her in his arms and ran his hand back through her hair caressingly, his eyes filled with warmth and admiration.

But Gina wasn't having any of it. Things needed settling here. "You mean there's more than one way to laugh at a person?" she asked incredulously.

"No," he said, but began to laugh again, shaking his head at her and hugging her even as she fought to get out of his arms.

"Let go of me, you bully!" she said, wriggling and pushing and trying her damnedest to escape, but not succeeding in the least.

"So I'm a bully, am I?"

"Yes."

"Hmm," he said thoughtfully. "That's not very good. Would you be willing to marry a bully?"

She stopped struggling and went as still as a sleeping cat. "What did you say?"

"I said being a bully wasn't a very good thing."

"Not that part!" she yelled. "The other!"

"Oh. You mean about marrying me?"

Her eyes filled up with tears, but she didn't even notice them. She simply stared into Colin's eyes, loving him more than she'd ever thought it was possible to love someone. "I'd marry you," she said softly, shakily. "I'd marry you in a minute, if you asked me."

"Knowing what you know about me?" he asked, sounding skeptical. "That I'm a slob? That I'm a natural pessimist? That I'm worried this won't work out between us?"

She reached out and ran her fingers over his face, tracing the lines at the corners of his eyes, the small dimple in his right cheek. "I love you, Colin," she said softly. "I don't have any choice in the matter. My heart stepped in and took over and here I am, in love with you so much I can't see straight. I know you've got faults, but so have I. Maybe that's what marriage is—accepting each other in spite of the faults and finding ways to live with each other, not giving up on each other, but fighting *for* each other, *making* it succeed."

"Oh, Gina," he said fervently, pulling her into his arms and hugging her hard, "I'm the luckiest man alive." He squeezed her tightly. "Marry me, Gina. Soon, before I do something stupid and let you get out of my life."

"If you want me in your life, that's where I want to be," she said softly, searching his eyes.

He nodded, taking a deep breath that seemed to symbolize his deep inner peace. "I want you," he said, his voice filled with certainty. "I never thought I'd find someone like you, but now I have and I'm going to grab you. I *do* love you, Gina, with all my heart. I want to break the old patterns and begin new ones, happy ones. I want to start seeing some of those silver linings. I want to share my life with you,

grow old with you, have babies with you. I want you forever, Gina.''

''Then I guess I'll marry you,'' she said, smiling through
her tears of joy.

He kissed her fervently, then just held her, gazing peace-
fully into the fire. Then he said, ''You ever think how
strange life is?''

''All the time,'' she said dryly, smiling softly.

''I mean, what if I hadn't got lost that day and had a flat
tire? What if you hadn't almost run me over? Maybe none
of this would have happened.''

''Maybe it was meant to happen.''

''Meant to?''

She shrugged. ''Yes, you know, like maybe our guardian
angels got together and figured out we were right for each
other and so they sort of arranged things.''

''Kind of a match made in heaven, in other words,'' he
said, grinning.

''Yes,'' she said, smiling back, radiant. ''Exactly. A
match made in heaven. . . .''

Somewhere overhead, two sighs were heard, then the soft
flutter of wings. ''I guess they'll be all right now, don't you
think?'' one voice said.

''It looks that way,'' said the other, ''but for a while there,
I was sure worried.''

''Yeah, me too.'' There was a soft giggle. ''You sure had
your hands full with *her*!''

''Her!'' said the other. ''It was *him*! He was the problem!''

''Oh, shut up and let's leave them alone. Looks like
they're getting into that mushy stuff, anyway.''

* * *

Lying on the rug, Gina frowned and turned to Colin, who was busy nuzzling her neck. "Did you hear something?"

"Nope, didn't hear a thing. What was it?"

"I don't know, kind of whispering and giggling and...and..." Gina frowned. "Kind of like *wings* fluttering."

"It's just our hearts you're hearing," Colin said, laughing softly.

Smiling, Gina nestled into Colin's arms. "Yeah, I guess you're right."

Overhead, an irate voice said, "Hearts, my halo! Those two fools don't even recognize angels hovering overhead when they hear them!"

"Oh, come *on*!" said the other irritably. "You're just as bad as she is. Let's get back to heaven." There was a soft chuckle. "Look. That's where *they* seem to be...."

Indeed, that's exactly where Gina and Colin were, and where they intended to stay.

* * * * *

ATTRACTIVE, SPACE SAVING BOOK RACK

Display your most prized novels on this handsome and sturdy book rack. The hand-rubbed walnut finish will blend into your library decor with quiet elegance, providing a practical organizer for your favorite hard-or soft-covered books.

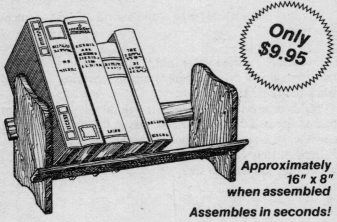

Only $9.95

Approximately 16" x 8" when assembled

Assembles in seconds!

To order, rush your name, address and zip code, along with a check or money order for $10.70* ($9.95 plus 75¢ postage and handling) payable to *Silhouette Books.*

Silhouette Books
Book Rack Offer
901 Fuhrmann Blvd.
P.O. Box 1396
Buffalo, NY 14269-1396

Offer not available in Canada.

BKR-2A

*New York and Iowa residents add appropriate sales tax.

In October
Silhouette Special Edition
becomes
more special than ever
as it premieres
its sophisticated new cover!

Look for six soul-satisfying novels
every month . . . from
Silhouette Special Edition

# Silhouette Desire

COMING
NEXT MONTH

#457 NIGHT CHILD—Ann Major
Part of the **Children of Destiny** trilogy. Years ago Julia Jackson had been kidnapped before young Kirk MacKay's eyes. Now an amazing turn of events offered him a second chance....

#458 CALL IT FATE—Christine Rimmer
Wealthy Reese Falconer had spurned Cassie Alden's awkward teenage advances. But when a twist of fate brought them together, he could finally take what he'd really wanted nine years before.

#459 NO HOLDS BARRED—Marley Morgan
The long-awaited prequel to *Just Joe*. When Cole Baron rescued an inebriated Jassy Creig from the honky-tonk bar, he knew there was one man she'd never be safe from—him!

#460 CHANTILLY LACE—Sally Goldenbaum
When Paul Forest investigated the mysterious pounding in his grandmother's attic, he didn't know which was more surprising—finding beautiful, dusty Rosie Hendricks...or his irresistible urge to kiss her.

#461 HIT MAN—Nancy Martin
Maggie Kincaid didn't trust Mick Spiderelli's fallen angel looks or hit man reputation, but her daughter was in danger. Soon taking care of the Kincaid women became Mick's particular specialty.

#462 DARK FIRE—Elizabeth Lowell
Cynthia McCall was thoroughly disillusioned with men *and* their motives until she met Trace Rawlings. The handsome guide was more man than she'd ever known—but could she trust her heart?

AVAILABLE NOW:

#451 DESTINY'S CHILD
Ann Major

#452 A MATCH MADE IN HEAVEN
Katherine Granger

#453 HIDE AND SEEK
Lass Small

#454 SMOOTH OPERATOR
Helen R. Myers

#455 THE PRINCESS AND THE PEA
Kathleen Korbel

#456 GYPSY MOON
Joyce Thies